Jimmy Jazz **III** Complete Works


1 House of the Unwed Mother

2 The Cadillac Tramps

3 The Sub

4 M-Theory

5 Rube Goldberg Suicide Machine

6 Where Life is Inappropriate

7 Home Despot

8 Nothing a Fire Can't Fix

9 This Ragged Muscle

10 The Book of Books

# M-THEORY

## STORIES BY JIMMY JAZZ

First Edition

To Shawn Nelson appeared in City Works 1998

Constipation appeared in Carbon 14 #13 1998

A Clean, Well-Lighted Bedroom Window appeared in Carbon 14 #15 1998

Going to the Mat appeared in City Works 1999

Less Thank Purple appeared in Fiction International 35 2002

Governed By Superstition appeared in City Works 2002

ISBN:1234567890123

Book Design: Jimmy Jazz

Garamond 3 & Avenir were used in the design of this book.

An unreleased version of this book titled The Symphony of Urban Decay was edited by Casey Kait.

Pirate Enclave Books

https://pirateenclave.square.site

# M-Theory 🖼 Stories

*If you rip off the fronts of houses, you'd find swine.*

*Uncle Charlie*

*We're living in a human zoo, the animals are me and you.*

*Sham 69*

# TABLE OF CONTENTS

# INTRODUCTION

When I was in third grade my mom went to the garage and built a rocket
ship, which she gave to my teacher. My teacher set it up in the classroom
as a reading fort; you could earn points and spend time in there with a
book. My mom liked to be out in the garage making things. Eventually,
she started a small business making children's tables and chairs shaped
like animals. My dad considered himself an artist and would spend a lot
of time, mostly weekends, painting in his studio. He'd even done some
landscape art in the front yard.

So if not inherent, my Do It Yourself sensibility was nurtured early. I spent
a lot of time in the 1980s making videos of punk rock shows. I sold some
of the tapes at Off the Record in San Diego. I was videotaping bands like
Black Flag who put out their own records and even created their own
touring networks. There were15-year-old kids like Scott Tied Down
putting on shows and other kids making zines.

So when I wrote my first books, it seemed natural to print and distribute
them myself. I'd heard Ian MacKaye of Dischord Records say since his
band got all the money from the sale of a record instead of the small
percentage a major label might pay, they didn't need to sell as many
records.

I liked this idea. I admired MacKaye's integrity, but also liked the control I
could have over my art. Publishers had editors. They made decisions
based on sales. I never wanted anyone to tell me what to write. In 1993 I
wrote three novels. I used my Macintosh Classic computer to layout the
pages and took them to Cal Copy where they charged a penny a page.
Penny dreadfuls! The books had a unique 5 x 11 size, all the text appeared on the right-hand side, so you had to flip it at the end. I cut the
pages from 8.5 x 11, drilled holes in the paper at my mom's woodshop
with her drill press, and sewed one big signature. The cover was printed
on 110 lbs. pink, yellow & grey card-stock with artwork by my friend
Patrick Haley.

Haley was doing his own DIY art, painting on cardboard boxes and showing the work in coffee houses where I would soon do spoken word shows.
I started at open mic at Java Joe's in Ocean Beach. I did one of my first
featured readings with Tamara Johnson at the Wikiup Café when she set
up readings at the Independent Music Seminar with Gary Hustwit. I met
all the best writers in town in one night. We marched over to The Live

Wire bar and I bought three pints with the money I'd earned reading poetry.

Gary Hustwit had started Incommunicado Press, which was publishing independent literature by Pleasant Gehman, Iris Berry, Nicole Panter, and Liz Belile. Belile gave me a chance to perform in six cities at Lollapalooza in 94 where I met exciting writers from all around the country. Incommunicado published my novel The Sub in 96 and I was doing readings in Los Angeles, Phoenix, Chicago, New York, Austin, San Francisco.

When Incommunicado moved from San Diego to New York and The Times mentioned a book by The Spacewürm, I didn't think I'd ever have to look for another publisher. Incommunicado was my City Lights, my Black Sparrow. I thought I could focus on writing and forget the business. Many of the writers I met, however, knew they had to be experts in the publishing industry. They knew the business, they knew agents, editors, publishers. They followed publishing trends like brokers follow the market. When everything fell apart, at the burst of the tech bubble, I didn't look for a new publisher. A literary agent told me to go write a long book and come back in a few years. I wrote a long book but never went back. Returning instead to my DIY roots.

In school, they tell you to put your stories in a drawer for a year before revising. Some of these have been biding time tucked away 30 years now. I wrote The Examined Life in a class at SDSU in 1989. I remember two things the professor said. "This story will never be published" and "Your writing reminds me of Proust." I didn't know who Proust was, but I listened to her criticism about the story and the cuts she suggested made it stronger. I'm still unsure what she meant about Proust. Do It Yourself, like auteur, is a misnomer. I rely on my friends who make art, make films, and make music to help me. I also rely on my readers.

Revising in 2020 felt like moving furniture around in an apartment you've lived in 20 years. Push that word over there by the window. Set that paragraph out on the curb. I believe the stories have held up, though you will be the true judge.

Jimmy Jazz 2020

# THREE DRUNK STORIES

## Jubilee Dunbar's Corridos

I was in San Francisco. It was the last week I was living there and I got hired by some club owner on Valentine's Day to sit outside an El Vez show in front of a fake cactus and cardboard coyote. El Vez is the Mexican Elvis. They gave me a sombrero to wear and asked me to play corridos on acoustic guitar. Payment was a bottle of Cuervo. The Cuervo went fast. The Cuervo was part of the setting. They wanted me to drink the tequila while playing to further denigrate Mexicans. I blacked out two songs into El Vez's set, woke up with an enormous bottle of water next to me… at home. Had a half-hour to get to work. Had to take the bus you know. Naturally, I was hungover. Thoroughly. Apparently… (at least according to my brother) the El-vettes [El Vez' go-go dancers] were carrying me around the club, Do you know who he belongs to? Since I was with El Vez they couldn't ditch me. My sister was singing with El Vez at the time. You know El Vez is my cousin, right? So, they were taking me home, I was living with my brother Baba, and on the way home I was trying to pick fights with the entire El Vez band. You LA geezer loser hacks will never amount to anything. You know how LA musicians are? LA rock guys. My sister calmed them down, so I didn't have to fight. I was five minutes late to work, which didn't matter so much because it was my last night before moving back to San Diego. I ran the meat saw at a catering place, the big rotary blade saw. After cutting myself a few times, I blame the hangover, I had to wrap my hands in tinfoil and Saran wrap to keep the blood off the meat. I commenced drinking copious amounts of OJ. The tequila was still in my system, a large amount of it anyway, so it was like making tequila sunrises in my stomach. I went to the bathroom and puked up this yummy tequila sunrise. Which wasn't bad, sweet stuff. If you're going to puke, this is the way to do it. Here I was with orange juice puke breath and tin foil on my hands. I ended up falling asleep in the cooler.

## Shindig's Worst Hangover

Worst hangover when I drunk with my guitar player. In the band called Dazzling Airbornes. After practice. Two days before the first show we gonna play. We are a lot of nervous. We start drinking at the bar eight o'clock after the practice. We came out at ten. Summertime hot night in Tokyo. We need more beer. We went to liquor store. We bought a gallon of beer. They selling beer by the gallon in Tokyo. A little keg. Do you know what keg is? We bought Early Times, American whisky, it's like Jack Daniel's thing, Bar-bon. Then we start drinking in my parents' house, 'til three o'clock in the morning. Only we had is chips, potato chips. We keep drinking drinking drinking. Suddenly after three o'clock, we start to make phone call to everybody in town we know. Drink and call is a big popular thing in Tokyo. Especially drunken teenagers. Drunk and smoking stoned teenager things. Hea hea hea hee. Remember I called you in America Jimmy Jazz. We also called San Francisco. We forgot which house was that. We called SeyMour in the Golden Hill. He wasn't home. Finally, we called the drummer's house. He was sleeping with his girls friend. We didn't care. We said WE ARE COMING WE ARE ON THE WAY TO YOUR HOUSE (in crazy cartoon drunk voice) PICK US UP AT TRAIN STATION. Then we hung up. We called million else's places, we don't remember. The next day feedback from the people we called. 'Hey fuck you Shindig what was that calling at three in the morning.' We apologized. We found out drummer came to the Shinjuku station, the biggest station of the Tokyo, like London station or New York station. He waited for two hours there. We told him we were coming to see him. Next day, we throw up like volcano. Volcano of Hawaii. The puke came out of my mouth like lava, that was red and green yellow brown some chunky some gooey ha ha ha ha, I don't know what the hell but there was some purple things, you see the blue, and inside of puke you can see something's moving. That made smelly that made my parents' house smells like... what? like what? 100-years-old bathroom of Balboa Park. Hangover whole day twenty-four hours plus twelve hours day after that. We had forty hours hangover.

And our show was sucks.

## Jimmy Jazz's Three Caballeros

Most of the best drunk stories, Cecil said, start Apparently I... Indubitably! SeyMour agreed. Three caballeros, three queer caballeros. I'm SeyMour, I'm Cecil, I'm Jimmy. Ha ha ha. When Cecil was in the Navy we used his visits as an excuse to get wild crazy drunk belligerent and sleazy. There was always some sleaze. Some seed. We would cruise to this place we called The Dairy Mart to goggle eyefuls of jiggling boobies. We would get drunk all day at SeyMour's girlfriend's apartment while she was at work and all night to the music of whatever band was playing at the club or on the car stereo. We spent time in Tijuana, of course, drunk, in and out of strip clubs and bars. One time a topless dancer straddled Cecil's lap. I think that was a dude, I said. No, it was a chick, he said raising a finger to inhale. SeyMour was always looking for pouch, which we stalked like a troop of broken kangaroos—limp dick drunk fumble-hop and slur-slobber after our jills as they left us in a cloud of scornful laughter.

Spanning the day I drank fifteen beers. Cecil paid. I would run to the bar with his money and pick up rounds by the six-pack. They let me have the cardboard case and everything which somebody ended up wearing as a silly drunk man's dunce beanie. We were standing in the middle of the dance floor amused by how doltish people looked boogying to the worn-out beat. The disco ball spinning lights across our numb faces. Maybe fifty bodies packed the dance floor tight. But it wasn't our music; it didn't move us, so we stood there, laughing.

I heard the DJ has a Circle Jerks record, go tell him to play it, Cecil said. SeyMour pushed through the crowd to schmooze the DJ and it turned out he was a friend of the artist Shawn Kerri who had designed the Circle Jerks logo. She'd given him the record, but he wouldn't play it. The bar was closing and, apparently, the sense I was Jerry Lee Lewis had taken possession of me. I was drawling in a southern accent singing, Great Balls of Fire. I was calling SeyMour "Elvis" and Cecil "John Cash" probably because he was buying the beer. SeyMour looked a bit like the young Elvis, with his coif, his charm, and his insatiable appetite for excess. I was fucked up staggering. I feared the lights were going out on consciousness but it was last call and the real-world lights in the bar had dimmed. We zombie-walked to the parking lot to look for my Toyota Corona. Somebody had left a pickup truck with the keys in, so Elvis, Cash, and I climbed in for a turn around the lot. We were looking through the cassettes. What is this shit? Cash said tossing one out the window. After a minute we abandoned

the truck close to where we picked it up, left the keys—
motor running.

Let's go Jerry Lee. A light breeze carried sea salt and decay-
ing kelp up from the beach. I can't drive, I can barely walk,
I said in the voice of The Killer. They tried to wrest the
keys from me physically, but I zipped my leather and said,
No, no no no. I had them gripped in my right fist and fell
balled armadillo-like on the asphalt. Cash was pounding on
me. *I shot a man in Reno*, I sang to myself. *Just to watch him
die.* I pulled out my Swiss army pocket knife and said, Back
off Johnny. Cash grabbed my wrist and wrested it free. They
were both whoop jump pile on like f'd up grease monkeys
gone chemical or electroshock experiment wild, tearing
back at the glib mad scientist me. I was determined in my
mad drunk brain not to let anyone, even The King, drive
my Toyota. They pounded, bounded. Whoo hoo hoo hoo!
I got up and stagger-leed to the Toyota. Goodness gra-
cious great balls on fire. Elvis pushed me, I lost balance
and fell back SPEAR into the corner of the bumper. Lay offa
my blue suede shoes. That hurts. Reflex trigger, spring-
loaded… I got up blind swinging drunk, clocked Elvis
across the eye with a closed left fist. Blood poured from his
unseamed forehead (the scar to be hidden by his eyebrow).

Cecil, we're leaving, he said.

I was laughing and crazy. Elvis was bleeding into his hands. He was calm. Cash and Presley walked away and I crawled into my Toyota. Drove it across the street in front of the tavern and went to sleep. Sometime during the night, I opened the door to puke. Vomit splashing in a green chunk pile on the street by the door. I went to sleep.

I had a wicked hangover. Some blurry guy flung the door to my car open. His dog snarled. I opened one eye. It must have been around seven because the sun was up. Too bright. I was dizzy sick with nausea. The guy screamed, Mother fucker, stealing car stereos… All I could think was, What kind of asshole would steal a car stereo and fall asleep on the street nearby? His dog was lapping up my puke. Fuck off, I mumbled pulling the door shut. I locked it and settled in sleep. I was out hot, sweating, dizzy. The warm California sun was coming on strong. I slept.

I don't know how much time went by –OCK KNOCK KNOCK! on the window. I looked up. Both eyes were able to open and sort of focus on the officer. I snapped awake. Still feeling sick.

Step out of the car please.

Two police cruisers had me blocked in. Twin cops hands on holstered guns. Put your hands on top of your head.

Do you have any weapons on you? the second cop asked. I strained to remember what happened to the knife as they patted me down.

I drank too much at Billy Bones tavern here in front of us and decided to sleep it off rather than drive home, I told them. Isn't that the right thing to do?

Do you know anything about this blood on the car? We walked around to the front side. The cops' hard-soled shoes clacked against the asphalt. SeyMour's blood was all over my white Toyota. Dark and dried.

No sir.

The cops left and I went back to sleep.

I found out later Elvis and John Cash met some girls. They took my drunk buddies, one bleeding into his hands, to the Denny's on Garnet and Mission and to their beach front condo. Cecil said he stuck his hand down one of the chick's pants.

# THE SYMPHONY OF URBAN DECAY

We lie awake in bed. Listening. Familiar sounds put me on edge. Jimmy's asleep or seems to be. Clem and his ladder woke me again. Four times a night after night he climbs up and onto the roof of his two-story apartment building, must be sixty feet looking down, to adjust a satellite dish. I'm not so afraid of him anymore, time being a great mediator. But his buddies scare me. One sleeps on the cement under the stairs. Desperation leaks from their talk like oil from my dad's Mustang. All manner of tweakers and misfits bang the door at night. Last Sunday, in the morning, early, this junkie-looking dude nodded off at the top of the stairs for about what must have been thirty minutes. He was young, eighteen if that. We thought for sure the wind would fell him like a tree, that he'd tumble like laundry in a blissful mangle of limbs. But he swayed fore and aft, to and fro, ebb and flow with his gaze fixed on something we couldn't see. Men with shell-shock in their eyes, blank-faced except fear in telltale lines pushed shopping carts up the block night and day. Clem was a collector. Whatever they could find in the alleys, out of dumpsters, on street corners, he would hand over cash. All this crap secreted away in his rooms: barstools and bicycle wheels, plumbing works, and busted umbrellas… You could see manikin limbs and a coat tree piled by the window.

One of his hobo friends wore one Nike and one Adidas taking endorsements from rival camps, wore stain-colored pants, and a polyester golf shirt. The hobo aesthetic says, Spare change? Deep indigence emerges from the Petri dish of the streets like bacteria. A new generation appears overnight. You start with any shirt any pants doesn't matter and let it go. Just let go. When you wear a uniform, as I have to at work, you feel like part of a team. Clem is way past that. His style has evolved beyond pants. You'll never see him in more than dirty blue silk underwear with his hairy ugly torso exposed and the crippled arteries of his legs affecting the way he walks. Every time I hear that ladder clank, I imagine an assault on our house. Up on the deck, smash the glass. You don't need to attend Juilliard to take the first chair in the symphony of urban decay. I must have dozed off… not sure how long… awoken by breaking glass.

Hey, wake up.

Hmmm? ya.

Wake up. I heard a noise.

Jimmy gets out of bed, shuffles to the window, presses his forehead against the glass trying to discern. His brow leaves an imprint. Sometimes I think he doesn't care about being a boyfriend. He could be more vigilant. He could put more effort into finding a steady career, so we could find a better place to live. The sound of metal twisting and glass breaking keeps repeating.

What is that? Is it moving closer? I think it's moving closer.

It's probably those kids who write Woptown Krazy Boyz on the wall. Maybe one of their boys got popped for graffiti and they're out smashing windshields for payback. The radio said a kid faced forty-eight years in prison for writing his name on the wall.

I went to check on our daughter, Ariadne. Climbed into bed with her. She's nine. I don't think she likes living here either. She's internalized our fears, the ones we got from TV. The ones where sick freaks predate and cruise in their hippie vans looking for kids. Jimmy says the perverts of the future will drive minivans. Ariadne knows our childhood was different, that times have changed, that we ran and played, that our parents had no idea where we were as long as we were home by dark. She knows it's not safe out there. She's snuggled up with one of her stuffties. Jimmy paces, straining to listen.

I'm going to investigate, he says.

Please stay out of it, I say exercising futility, regretting waking him.

It'll be okay, I'll take the car, the noises seem to be coming from the other block. I can't sleep without knowing.

Jimmy deadbolts the front door on his way out. He rattles the knob to see if it's secure. The warmth of my daughter's body huddling into mine soothes my nerves. In the second minute, I picture Jimmy meeting the gangbangers.

Whachu looking at home-boy?

A frustrated little shit so bored he has to disturb the peace?

This would be Jimmy's failed attempt to connect. He wants to help. He wants to understand where the kids come from. Poverty is a sorry basis for common ground. Jimmy's great grandfather emigrated to this country with hope in his seabag around 1880. He sailed logging ships out of Sweden to Boston. A tall tale about his great-great-grandfather had him swept off his ship by a stormy sea to have a second wave place him back on deck. A "miracle" they called it. His grandma liked to say the family was blessed. His parents bought homes, bought cars. Jimmy managed to get to a university and finish, but we've been sliding back to poverty with a hundred dollars in the bank and none under the mattress.

Jimmy says he wants to volunteer at the youth center. He thinks if he can get the kids to write poetry, it might help channel their destructive energy. I think it will add to their frustration. Especially if a kid turns out to be a good writer. Bohemian poverty isn't all it's cracked up to be. With luck, his audience will say they understand him after suicide.

If we lived in a better area and Jimmy had a full-time job to occupy his mind, I think we might have a shot at happiness. A normal life. All I want is to be able to sleep at night. [Crrrrunncchh.] Oh my god. The sound feels so close. That was probably our car windshield. Stupid kids got tired of throwing eggs at us and moved to bricks. Jimmy was a high school teacher until he cracked. He took it personally when the kids ditched class or got sent to juvie. It was too much. He stopped brushing his teeth. It was terrible. He took it personally when they did dumb things like pass bags of weed around. He thought it was his fault instead of just his job. If he can find a new career, everything will be alright. I know it.

The streets are devoid of human life. All I've seen so far is a possum playing dead with his entrails baked on the asphalt. The glowing eyes of stray cats cower behind parked car tires. A cat darts in front of me, but I'm cruising slow, so it reaches a tentative safety on the other side of the street. I drove down Maple and circled around the block. It's all quiet here on Curlew. This block is mostly Mexican immigrant families while ours seems peopled with Europeans. We the Northern Euros, aka Vikings, are more recent immigrants to the neighborhood, though the Italians have been here as long as the fishing industry. And the Portuguese. I worry about gentrification. Like traffic, most people think it's caused by everybody else. I can walk to The Casbah, check out whatever band happens to be playing. I can get in free some nights, once in a while someone will buy me a drink.

The rent's cheap. We expect cheap as we accept the planes coming in low to land every three minutes and the freeway blowing continuous black soot through our windows. Watching the neighborhood change is never easy. The new whites don't buy produce from Pedro's Vegetable Truck, so pretty soon it won't be feasible for Pedro to stop here. When my own personal familia blanca moved in, Pedro came twice a day. The neighborhood kids would mob the van for peaches and strawberries. Or a sack of tomatoes with salt. Pedro doesn't even stop on our block now. News reported hepatitis germs on Mexican strawberries that the city schools bought, which sucks for a small businessman like Pedro. All the kids who lived here when we moved in have moved on. The school district calls it a "transient" population, parents move where they can find work. When we first moved in, the one-bedroom apartment next to us had eight people living in it. The apartment downstairs housed a migrant family, on the move, without furniture. I saw them, through the busted blind, sleeping on the floor. They moved on a few days later.

The big family upstairs let their trash blow off the balcony into our yard. I picked up egg cartons and Farmer John sausage wrappers in the morning. The parents and older siblings worked leaving the smaller children with their grandmother. Her call, Niño-o-os! echoed, as she leaned on her squeaky-wheeled walker. I have yet to see her traverse the stairs.

We communicated by smiles and gestures and my daughter played ball with one of their boys. He would toss it down from the balcony and Ariadne would try to hurl it up. It was my job to get the ball off the roof. They moved out in the middle of the night. The apartment was thrashed. The landlord was a tight bastard who wouldn't fix anything, wanted to unload the building. Consequently, the roof leaked and the plumbing reverberated and the heater didn't heat. Subsequently, the piece of shit sold the place, a lucky day, to a guy with a real beating heart and loose wallet. He turned out to be a first-rate confidence man—never paying the bank. He lived rent-free and collected rent on the other units for a year before he disappeared in the middle of the night. I liked the guy. He painted the walls and fixed the heater. He paid to fix our refrigerator. He told us he played with The Jazz Messengers, sat in with Miles Davis once. He liked to smoke while he told stories and would light one with one in the ashtray.

I can't seem to find the source of the noise. I drive where I thought it was, but it's a sound mirage. A ventriloquist's trick.

As I turn the car up Brant Street, where we live, I can see Alaska has turned on the lights. She always does when I'm out. I know she doesn't like living here, though her pleas to move on up wax and wane in synch with her menstrual cycle. I don't want to be one of those assholes who dismisses a lady's true feelings about something as PMS. But she says something different every week. Truth is I'll use what I can to enforce the status quo. I love our house which has a fantastic view of the harbor and the skyline. Tonight the buildings are lit like jewels. An asset that inspires. I'm not someone who accepts change with dignity. I've been wearing the same clothes for thirteen years, at least partly because I like them. I got most of them at thrift shops anyway, so going out of style is not an option. They either never were in style or have come in and gone out and come back. Even though I've gained weight, around the middle especially, and my pants don't fit like I was twenty, I wear them. It's easy to put on weight. A couple of beers every day. More sitting. I've got a peanut butter sandwich habit after dinner. Life is good.

With the lights on I can make out the pink letters on THE CLASH poster in my living room. Our mini-blinds have been busted since day one. It was busted shut or busted open, so we went for open. The sun destroys everything eventually. A security light illuminates the dead plants in our flower boxes. I should- [Crunnchhh.] Shit. There's that fucking noise. And there's that crazy fucker we call Clem with his ladder climbing on the roof in his boxer shorts to adjust the satellite dish. What the hell is so good on television to hassle with your life every night? I've seen him up there in lightning storms, high winds, and savage heat.

I think the sound that drove me out here is coming from two blocks up. My car moves on, silently, like a police cruiser. I've never been the Neighborhood Watch type, Big Brother scares me. And I never liked those Guardian Angels with the military berets. Fucking vigilante narks. I believe there is an acceptable level of crime. I understand what it means to be desperate. If I didn't have Alaska and Ariadne, I can't say where I'd be. The law of the stomach. The arbitrary rules set up to keep the rich rich and the poor down can't suppress it. I can't go back in until I find the noise.

When we first moved here, the 'hood seemed scary. The beat condition of the houses, the sharp edge on the neighbors, the homeless guys digging fruitlessly through our trash for recyclables. I take our recyclables to the dump to get cash, which is sad because it cuts into a margin of safety for our industrious bums. That much less relief into their stomachs or veins. I think those "bums" who collect cans are modern-day heroes doing more to save the world from dawn 'til dusk than most of us. They walk without footprints, consuming little, reducing waste, and mollifying landfills. I think if Alaska talked with some of the neighbors her fear would mellow. Like the psycho-loco-cholo is Beto the mechanic. And one of the bums is Ali, a bona fide Rastafari trying to be cool and get by. He's too stoned to fuck with anyone. These are our crazy people. Downgraded from frightening to eccentric. Some fear is healthy. Alaska should be afraid of that kook who yelled, Shut up and drink your coffee! when she was walking Ariadne to school.

I drove down Ivy, turning left instead of right. [Crunchhh!] It's louder so I know I'm going the right way. Up on the freeway which passes over our neighborhood, I see the flashing lights of a cop car. Even though there's no one around I'm wary of getting out of the car. I can see the headlights of the cars above on the graffitied freeway. I time the oncoming lights with the sound, and it's clear something made of glass and metal fell on the road and the passing cars are running over it.

Aaagghh! Shit. Shit. Shit. Where is Jimmy? That fucking asshole. Ariadne get back in bed. Shut the door. Ooogh. I was curled up with Ariadne, heard a noise, so came to check it out. Once I got to the window I could see it was just Clem with his aluminum ladder. I watched him climb up on his roof. That was when this giant roach flew at me. It came straight at me like it was going for my throat. Fffff. It's sitting on the TV; it's about four inches long. Brown. All slimy like it came from the sewer. Ewwww! Shit. Here it comes. That fucking asshole Jimmy. Where the fuck is he? Ariadne open the door! I knock softly trying to remain calm. But the giant bug is coming at me. Open the door! The door opens. I slam it. I think I hear the roach thump against the door. Living here is like living in a horror movie. I hate this place. It's never clean. I sweep every day. I mop the kitchen. An hour later it's dirty. It's charming. I'll live in new over charming in a heartbeat. That fucking ass Jimmy.

That's it, Ariadne, we're telling your father it's time to move. I've had it.

I don't like bugs mom. Dad said not to use the word Hate but I think I hate bugs. Can we live somewhere without bugs? Dad says new houses have more bugs because most bugs don't like to live in drafty places. What's drafty?

In your father's case, it's like daffy.

Like Daffy Duck?

They used to call him Drafty Duck.

I can't get to sleep with the light on mom.

Well, I can't sleep with the light off Booboo.

Dad says we have to compromise.

Close your eyes—how's that for compromise? It must have been okay because Ariadne falls asleep within minutes. We're trapped in the bedroom. I'm wearing my nightgown, which I think is too sheer and too sexy for my thirty-two-year-old body. Even though Jimmy bought it for my twenty-one-year-old body, he says I rock it. I guess that shows how long we've been together. Why can't I use the money I work for to buy new clothes once in a while? Shit. The tears are running down my cheeks. I can't handle stress. Shit. [Clank a clank.] What the fuck is that noise now? I ponder opening the bedroom door to check it out, but if the roach jumps at me my heart will stop.

I guess I should get home. It would be nice to pop down to the pub and see if anyone's hanging out after hours. A pint would help me sleep. It's late though. The corner store closed hours ago. There's a 7-Eleven on Fifth, but they lock the liquor case at two. Usually, I keep a bottle of wine at home, but money has been tight. How can all those unemployed men afford to sit around at The Board Room or The Waterfront drinking schooners all day? Since I can't see anything I might as well go home.

Someone's knocking on the door. Jimmy must have forgotten his house key. I open Ariadne's bedroom door slowly. There is a calm feeling in the room, placid, like the morning harbor. Like the cooling air at sunset. It sounds like Jimmy. I don't see the roach. [knock, knock] The knocking is coming from the deck door. I should let Jimmy rot out there. A night in the doghouse might do him some good. The roach takes off from its perch on the telephone table. Its wings beat frantic. Coming straight at me. Before I can hop back in the bedroom, I hear the deck door clatter and I see the bug circle and land on the telephone. I shut the bedroom door. This is too much. Ariadne is asleep with her mouth open like her father.

I can't find a space on our street. When we first moved in a lot of the neighbors rode city busses. I'd see them at the stop every morning. There was never a hard time finding a spot. It's become a parking nightmare. I see the lights are still on. Clem's ladder isn't propped against his building. He must be settled in for a show, hopefully with clear reception. Nothing. I'm going to have to park on the next block.

As I laid down with Ariadne, it sounds like Jimmy was able to get in. Get the roach. Get the roach, it's by the phone. I hear a newspaper rolling. [whap!] Sounds like he clobbered it. I'm so tired. Relieved though. That's funny, he usually catches the slimy monsters and throws them outside.

A teenager is running up the street. He's wearing all black. He's got what looks like a car stereo in one hand. I don't think he sees me. At the top of the street I can see the beam from a police searchlight. The kid ran through somebody's backyard and came out on this street. As he gets closer I recognize him. He's usually hanging out a few blocks away with friends, drinking malt liquor. This is the first time I've seen him with his shades off. He jumps over a hedge and lays low. As the prowl car hits this street the light shines over his hiding spot. The kid stays cool and undetected. I duck as the light comes at me. It lights up the car and moves on. When I look up I see the cop driving away. I love this neighborhood.

Jimmy… did you get the bug? It's too quiet out there. I want to sleep, but I decide to take a look. I get up, it feels chillier now. I open the door slowly. The first thing I see is the big roach on its back—dead on the floor. The deck door is open. Jimmy must have gone out to catch the view. He's raves about the view. [click ick ick] Wait, that sounds like the key in the front door. Jimmy walks in. He has a stupid grin on his face, like he got his birthday blow job.

What are you doing? I ask.

Nothin'. The noise was something that fell off a truck on the freeway. Cars keep running it over. Nothing to worry about. He takes off his jacket. He looks at the dead bug on the floor. He rubs his bare arms like he's got a chill. Why have you got the deck door open? Jimmy pulls it shut.

We hear another clanking. Looking out the window I see Clem propping his ladder up to his roof to adjust the satellite dish. He's still wearing that dirty blue underwear. Half way up the ladder he pauses, turns his thick hairy neck and looks right at me. I step back from the window.

I walk into the bedroom, pull on my faux fur coat. I take the car keys, pick up Ariadne and she snatches her stuffed Dalmatian. The two of us are going to my dad's house in the suburbs.

# A CLEAN, WELL-LIGHTED BEDROOM WINDOW

I was walking down the path that leads to my house when I accidentally, mind you, saw my neighbor getting fucked from behind by a tall man. The mini-blinds on her window were shut, evening had fallen, and the light was on in her room. As luck would have it the blinds were off-kilter, open just enough. Captivating as the early 20th century Nickelodeon pictures flashing on the eye.

Today you are witness to a moment of clarity. A human kind of beauty so vivid as to exist beyond interpretation. A realism rather than the usual persistence of vision. My neighbor's exotic naked body stretching across the eyeball, as a leopard ready to leap. Her sleek fur tuned for precision. The muscles undulating. Purrrr. Her honeyed face writhing with passion. Her smooth skin, like that of a wet seal or porpoise. The man's palms on her hips. He has extraordinary hands with thick fingers. The tower of man pumping from behind. A faceless derrick working through the night. His face cropped by the window. Fingers like greasy sausages slip around her clit. Pubic hairs light and fragrant, an aroma therapy like fresh cut grass. The rhythmic pumping, the endless humping. His hands go wild! Cry out! They scream. Urge. But this is a silent movie. The sexual nature of beasts heated. To see this, by accident mind you, in passing a window, without breaking stride, proves emotional shock triggers memory and stimulates learning. My usual faulty mind took a picture. I learned her trunk, memorized each nipple, the curve of the hip, the pout on the lip, the subtle indentation of her well-tanned pinkly-fresh-pierced bellybutton. Each pump, the force of every hump calculated, stored in the retrievable memory folds of my gray matter.

There was nothing to do but walk the remaining sixty feet to my house and jerk off. With the anxious sperm out of my system, it would be easier to contemplate the next time I would have to face my neighbor, even though we just say 'Hi' or 'How's it going?' in passing. Though there was that ride she gave to the auto parts store when my car broke down. What do I say now that I've seen? I grew afraid our meetings would be charged with this stored sexual angst. Were I to divulge my felix culpa, my happy fault, she might think I was a cad. Do people still use the word cad? A sociopath. She would think I was some kind of sociopath. I decided to play it cool, not worry, let it pass.

I picked up a zine. I refried pintos and cooked rice for dinner. I did ordinary things. Against the light of what I had witnessed, everything seemed ordinary and mundane. If the rest of my life had to be visualized in this red light district, the light from my neighbor's sexual heat, the light from her bedroom window, how could I go on?

It was the window theater where I'd seen my ex-neighbor, Billy, in the constricting grasp of depression, like a vice on his skull easing his eyeballs out of the sockets, trying to commit suicide with two bottles of pills in his gut, two six-packs of beer catalyzing the active ingredients in a bad way, burning all his fuses in a screaming spastic foaming fit. He's gone now. He moved. His one-man show replaced by this peepshow.

But I thought What bliss! What rose-colored glasses! Every time I closed my eyes the scene replayed. My cock got hard, I jerked off, the sperm plowed into my palm. I wiped the main globule on a crumpled cloud of toilet paper and tossed it into the toilet. I flushed, because semen leaves recognizable bubbles on the surface of the water. I waddled over, hoisted my penis into the sink and washed the spermy residue down the drain.

What if someone looked in my bathroom window while I did that? Hey, what's that guy doing with his dick in the sink? I decided to live in that moment. Every action, every thought should be tinted—even influenced—by this most profound voyeuristic experience.

It was clear I could never be that tower of man pumping on my neighbor. The face of the tower had been hidden above the frame of the window, but even replacing my own face for his in the fantasy replay of the event seemed impossible.

I have a girlfriend who lives with me. We've been together ten years. More than ten years. We are happy. Well, I'm happy, she just informed me that she's not. Thinks the neighborhood is going down hill. Our sex life would be described by most people as adequate. She wishes I would be a better communicator and I wish she gave head more frequently.

She was at work when all this happened. She works at the San Diego Zoo, one of the world's prestigious zoos, a place of successful captive breeding and so many tourist dollars spent.

On our last excursion to the zoo, I thought it would be funny to wear matching overalls as we walked around the exhibits. She was afraid her coworkers might laugh. Later that day I witnessed intercourse between a male and female Szechuan takin. A takin is a beast like a bull or a water buffalo, except smaller. And shaggier. Its hypodermic sharp horns protrude from the skull perpendicular to the takin's body. As I replay that scene, the male takin is replaced by the tower of man. He is plodding away at the rump of the female takin, yet he's wearing my overalls. And the female takin transmogrifies into the form of my neighbor.

The night of the incident my girlfriend entered the house in a manic state. Her heart beat rapid. Lungs heaving in out in. Her left hand poised on her chest like she wanted to speak. I felt she had witnessed something "incredible" on the path between the street and our house. The look on her face reminded me of the quivering pout on my neighbor's sex lips.

What's the matter? I asked.

She took a second to compose her breath, spoke nervously, As I was walking down the path, I was startled by an old man.

An old man?

Yeah, he came out as I came in. You know how I make noise before I walk down the path because I'm afraid of the skunk…

We live in an urban setting in a house under the flight path. If the 767s didn't roll in at all hours we might complain about the freeway. Yet, we share our yard with skunks, possums, stray cats and other wild creatures. Too often the skunk is waiting on the path which leads to the house. His or her tail poised defensively, but exotically beautiful like… like the downy pubic hair of my neighbor.

We decided to go out on the path and investigate. As we got to the neighbor's bedroom window, I saw the light on inside. A large brick had been set up in front of the window. It probably weighed twenty-five pounds. I stood up on it. It provided an even better view of my neighbor's room.

I bet that guy was looking through Jill's window, I said without thinking.

What makes you think that?

Hmm. Should I fess up?

The more I think about it, the more I think that guy was looking through Jill's window, I stammered, thinking repetition would buy time.

We should tell Jill a pervert was looking through her window.

I'm not sure what my face looked like.

I'm not so sure, I said. I saw Jill and, uh, some guy, having sex through that window, earlier. I confessed the story in detail (leaving out the part where I had to jerk off). She listened, intently—finding some humor, yet concerned about this dirty peeper.

I've never seen you embarrassed, she said.

I'm not embarrassed, I don't get embarrassed. I'd feel like, uh, a hypocrite, I said.

At that point I lifted the brick. I had to use both hands, lifting with my legs, of course. I heaved it into the bushes, out of sight, but by no means gone.

# MASTURBATION THEORY

*When you feel a revolutionary uprising in your system, get your Vendome Column down some other way—don't jerk it down.*

*Twain from Some Thoughts on the Science of Onanism*

*I use my left hand to make masturbation a creative act.*

*McBean from Masturbating on the Right Side of the Brain*

Wake up too early, get dressed, pack the minivan, dress the kid for school, hair combed, Kool-Aid™ smile removed, heat water, mix formula, feed baby, at six-thirty the nanny arrives. She's buoyant, twenty-two, cellulite-free, has thick hair. She's been working for my cousin for about two months. The nanny makes a peanut butter sandwich and puts four Oreos™ in a Ziplock™ for my nephew, slyly unscrewing one for herself scraping the cream with her front teeth like an adult might scrape the deep green leaf of an artichoke. Robert, the husband usually leaves first in the morning. I'm visiting my cousin Agnes in Irvine, California.

We're sitting in the metallic mirage blue minivan. It's idling. It's a new van. Another payment. Added to the house payment, her school tuition, and the emergency room bill from when her son was hit in the pelvis with a baseball. And the nanny's salary. The husband is going to ride his new motorcycle to work. He came home one day last month and said, Honey, to my cousin. Honey, I bought a motorcycle. No discussion, no heads up, no democratic decency. He has an hour-plus commute and says the bike will make the trip enjoyable. This he calls logic.

I'll see you girls later. Robert calls us 'girls' even though Agnes is almost forty and I'm thirty-two-and-a-half. I forgot to take out the trash, he says going back into the house and closing the front door. Whoever thought getting out that door in the morning could be so hectic? My cousin has a finger in her mouth. Nail-biter. Polish eater. A burgundy flake is stuck to her lipstick. I decide not to say anything. She was sensitive when we were kids. She's bitten her nails as far back as I remember, chewing until the tips of her fingers turn blue-black.

Still, my cousin seems to be aging with dignity. She looks good for someone who popped out two kids and is pushing forty like a boulder uphill though she won't admit she dyes her hair like I have since thirty to cover a score of silver filaments. Agnes shuts off the engine. We wait in the driveway.

What's wrong?

It's Robert, Agnes says. He's been in there too long.

Are you worried about the nanny? I ask in a tone meant to imply joking. Robert seems like a pretty typical aging male. Receding hair gone gray, matrix of wrinkles, crosshatches of stress. His physique isn't bad. It isn't great, but it isn't bad.

Maybe, Agnes says. You can't trust any man not to diddle the nanny. She gets out of the van. I'm going to find out what he's up to. That word diddle made the whole thing sound ridiculous. Robert? A diddler? Absurd. She goes through the side gate around the back of the house to spy. Meanwhile, Robert steps out the front door. He walks up to the van. I look into his eyes for a glint of infidelity. I try to picture the nanny; does she seem too cheerful?

Hey Al, where's Agnes?

I think she went around back to check on the dog, I say. Robert disappears through the side gate. I can see the dog lumber up and jump on his ironed slacks. He thumps the shaggy mutt's chest with his knee, brushes his pants with his hand, wipes the hand on his pants. In a minute Agnes and Robert emerge side by side. He gets on his motorcycle, it starts easily, he waves and rides off. Agnes gets in the van. We're still sitting in the driveway.

He caught me looking in the window.

You're not suspicious of Robert? I ask.

Oh… what if he never even thought that way about the nanny and my spy mission planted the idea?

I'm not sure what to say. I want to think she's crazy. I couldn't help thinking, though, how perfect the nanny's skin. And where was that trash he went back to get?

Out of the blue sky like a crow dropping on a cat to steal fur for its nest Agnes says, Robert doesn't like to have sex.

A man who doesn't like sex? That's hard to believe, I say intending pun.

If I tell you this, you have to promise not to tell anyone, my cousin whispers. Her gaze hits the rear-view mirror, clicks to the side mirror.

I promise, I say softly, wondering why we need to whisper.

You can't even tell Jimmy, because when a man learns certain "things" about another man, he looks at him differently, my cousin says.

Jimmy is my boyfriend. We've been together thirteen years. And for thirteen years he's been in a constant state of arousal. If I give it to him, he wants it that same night, and the next day and the next. I don't really need it like that. Maybe he should date my cousin and I should move in with Robert. They have such a beautiful house. And furniture. My cousin has great furniture.

Agnes says, The one thing I hate about moving is I have to drill a new hole in the bathroom door.

Wait. What? I say. She turns the key, the engine rattles to action.

Drill a hole, she says. Her eyes glance left, hit the side mirror, fix on me. I had this idea Robert was masturbating instead of having sex. And sure enough, I caught him doing it, in the shower. He loves to whack that thing more than he likes me. He lathers it and strokes it. I can't remember the last time he lathered and stroked me. Agnes' fingers slide along the line of the shoulder restraint adjusting it between her breasts. He sings while he's doing it. Do you think he sings while we're doing it? Hell no. I've been drilling holes in the bathroom door and watching out for him to whack off for ten years. At first, I marked the days he masturbated and compared them to the days we had sex. On the days he pleasures himself, he won't pleasure me. On the days he doesn't, we do. Understand? I must have shaken my head. If I see him through the hole whacking off, I interrupt.

I don't know how to react. I hesitate. We still haven't left the driveway. Feeling like I have to say something I say, Um. Jimmy masturbates too. But...uh it makes him hornier. The muscles in my face feel wrong. Why am I in this conversation?

What size drill bit did you use on the bathroom door? Agnes asks as if Drill and Spy were a national pastime. As if looking through a hole in the bathroom door was as mundane as a love scene in a Hollywood movie.

Um, I don't make a hole. He jerks off in front of me. I recall the time Jimmy squirted semen into my palm when I was asleep and tickled my nose with a feather. He didn't get any real sex for a month. Another time he mixed his masturbated sperm with some white paint, his runny snot with green, and his blood with red to paint a self-portrait. I don't share my anecdotes. I stay quiet, waiting for my cousin to pull out of the driveway. Sex is such a strange thing. I'm afraid if I tell Agnes about the man I live with, she might look at me differently.

The next time we're all together is Thanksgiving. The day runs its course without event until Robert challenges Jimmy to arm wrestle. The TV is on in the background. My dad is watching football. My mom is sitting on the couch whispering to her sister, Agnes's mom, about some remembrance of childhood. Jimmy clears the dishes from the extended dinner table and Robert hauls a platter holding the turkey remains into the kitchen. Spatters of cranberry sauce and gravy droplets mark the terrain. The boys clasp palms establishing their grip.

Go, Agnes says. The muscles in their forearms strain so hard I think their heads may burst like overripe tomatoes. Agnes watches and I can see she's thinking about sex. The tip of her tongue pushes out the corner of her pursed lips. Her man surges. Jimmy's hand almost touches, but he counters leveling it. The boys exude squat grunts. Barred teeth clench tighter. The sweat glistens like sea foam on ebbing hairlines. Each looks like he has something to prove. Agnes' porn star face is cracking me up. She's in silver screen ecstasy.

You told Jimmy about Robert masturbating instead of fucking, didn't you? my cousin says.

And you told Robert about Jimmy masturbating and trying to fuck more, I say.

She smiles folding her arms across her chest. We stand watching our boys, shaking violently, eye to eye, shoulder to shoulder, neither willing to secede. Agnes gnaws a fingernail. Do you think they'll have anything left for us?

I imagine so.

# CONSTIPATION

uuuuunnngggk. uh. uuuuunnngggk. uh. Constipated. When I finally pushed the piece of shit outta my ass I was surprised to see a human finger sink to the bottom of the toilet. It was brown and shitty with wispy tendrils flailing, but clearly a finger. The nail trimmed close. Cuticles pushed back. Brazened knuckles. My first impulse was of course to wipe and flush the whole business down the toilet.

The better part of it was already out of my system. The image of the object in the toilet could be erased, but could I forget how it got there? I decided not to flush. I got up, waddled out of the bathroom, pants around ankles, residue of shit hanging on my ass. Nobody else was home. I hopped into the kitchen. I searched the cupboard and found the salad tongs. I was hungry. I washed my hands at the kitchen sink, hopped over to the rack. Stowed tongs under armpit. Peanut butter. Unscrewed. Opened fridge. Where's the strawberry jam? Searched, couldn't find it, searched. Found jam and tortillas. Cooked the tortilla over the gas burner on the stove until it bubbled in brown flaky spots. Hopped over to the flatware drawer. Dropped the tongs on the tile. Got a spoon. Scooped one peanut butter glob onto a tortilla. Licked spoon clean. Dipped the spoon into the strawberry jam. Applied the jam. Took one large bite of pb & j burrito. Put the spoon in the sink. Picked up the tongs. Hopped back to the bathroom jamming second and final bite into mouth.

A kid in grade school said I was gross for eating an apple at the urinal. I shook my pisser with one hand and held the apple with the other. I've been more conscious of eating in the bathroom. I stood in the hall for a minute, pants down, chewing.

I hesitated with the tongs over the water. The finger rested at the bottom of the bowl. Teri would freak. She wouldn't even let me scoop our live goldfish out of its bowl with the soup ladle when I needed to change the water. Teri's my wife. We're shacked up six years. I've learned to put the seat on this toilet down. The peanut butter spoon licking thing really bugs her. We swap spit and other fluids. I eat her out and her fluid dries on my face. Do I complain? The tongs went into the water. I held the finger over the bowl and let most of the water drip off. It smells like shit. Suddenly I had to shit. I sat. I shat holding the rotten finger at arm's length. As I shifted the tongs to get a new roll of toilet paper, the finger dropped on the floor. It rolled over one turn and stopped.

I wiped. I hopped over to the sink. Washed hands. Pulled up pants. Buckled belt. People who pull up their pants before washing have shit on their belt buckles. I picked up the finger with the tongs and held it under the hot water. The brown whirlpool in the basin eventually ran clear. The finger looked even more like a finger though green, rotten, and still smelling like I pulled it from my butt.

Back in the kitchen, I packed the finger in a Tupperware. I put the tongs in the sink next to the peanut butter spoon. On the bridge to the house, I heard footsteps, a key in the lock. Hi honey, can you help me bring in the groceries, Teri requested.

Sure thing babe. I put the Tupperware in the fridge and hustled out to the car.

It's time to pick up Timpany at school, can you do it? I'm beat, she said.

I looked around for my keys. Found them on the floor in the hall. Out the door. In the car. Drove to the school. Traffic sucks. I was going to be late.

Timpany was not in front of the school. I parallel parked across the street in a red curb. Traffic seemed lighter than usual, but I still had to wait for a truck and a blue minivan to pass before crossing the street. I entered the school. I walked down the empty hall. My footsteps echoed. The classroom was dark. I tried the door, but it was locked. It appeared the teacher had gone home. I went to the office.

Hello Mr. Burns, rang a voice behind me. It was the kooky librarian. Your Timpany is so sweet, she said. My daughter is five. This is her fourth month of kindergarten. I went into the office. The secretary was busy filing papers, talking on the phone, and chewing gum.

Excuse me. Have you seen Timpany?

No, she said curtly. I got worried. I looked out at the playground. Several kids hung on the monkey bars. A group of third-grade girls chased a boy on roller blades across the blacktop. No Timpany.

I stepped back into the hall. I must have looked crazed with worry.

Is something wrong Mr. Burns? the librarian asked.

Yes, I can't find Timpany. I was supposed to pick her up.

School let out early today, Tuesday half day, remember? I was stunned. A surge of panic shot from where my prehensile tail was amputated by evolution, up my spine, into my brain. Something like the precursor to tears hit me in the stomach. I wanted to puke.

Where is she? I said harshly. The librarian smiled stupidly.

Oh her uncle picked her up.

Her uncle? What uncle?

Her uncle with the note from Timpany's mother. He picked her up on time. They left in his van.

His van? I was crazed. My fist contracted and I wrapped my forehead with the bony blue knuckles [thump]. The librarian was slow to sense the tension. Did you notice anything strange about this uncle?

No, she said, still smiling dumbly. I didn't know what to do. I felt an anxious tension in my fingers. Like I wanted to strangle the librarian. Oh! she recalled suddenly. He did have a heavy gauze bandage on his hand. Her pupils followed my rising hands like radar. A rational fear brought the rest of her thought forth one word at a time. Like, his, finger, had, been, chopped, off. My hands fell. It made sense.

I turned without saying another word to the librarian. I ran out the door, crossed the street without looking, heard the screech of tires and faint curses in a male voice as I leaped into my car, fumbled for the keys, squealed the tires and sped home.

My parking space was blocked by the garbage truck. The garbage man took too much time emptying the cans. He pulled the lever at the back of the truck and crushed the trash [uuuuunnngggk]. I left the car in the middle of the street. My feet sounded heavy on the wooden bridge. I tried to force the wrong key into the lock, eventually opening the door.

Any phone calls? I blurted trying to conceal the nervousness I was feeling. Teri looked at me. She was putting away the groceries. I noticed she washed the dishes.

I cleaned out the refrigerator. There was a lot of gross old food, she said. Where's Timpany? [ring] The phone. I picked it up. My hand was shaking.

I want my finger.

I heard Timpany's tiny voice singing in the background. Sing a song of six pence, a pocket full of rye, four and twenty blackbirds, baked in a pie...

I ran to the fridge. It was packed with the new groceries. Two gallons of milk, beer, coffee, juice... I looked over at the sink and saw the Tupperware. I checked the trash can. A fresh clean empty white plastic bag lined it. I looked out the window. The garbage truck had driven off. The street was quiet. I don't have it, I said to the man.

I don't care what condition it's in, I want it back.

I don't have it. Buh...

[Click, unnnnnnnnnnnnnnnnnnn...]

Police. Statements. Panic. Tears. Blame. Self-despising. Depression. Ponder suicide? We went through the steps of grief and had given up hope, when the familiar patter of feet on the bridge walk sent us rushing to the door. I flung it open as the little hand began its knock. As soon as she saw me Timpany teared up, as she did with a skinned knee or simple boo boo. I picked her up and crushed her to my body. Her mother burst out in hysterical tears of joy. At first glance Timpany appeared in perfect order. Then we both saw a gap in space. The middle finger on her left hand was missing.

Daddy, why did uncle Jimmy cut off my finger? Pregnant pause. I asked him and he said you'd tell me, Timpany said in her tiny five-year-old voice.

I don't know sweetheart.

Teri read the lie in my voice, she could read me like the deaf read lips. The lie was like a fart in an elevator though the truth was stuck in my belly.

I don't know, I sputtered, I'm so glad so glad so glad to have you back. My heart beat so hard I thought it would break my ribs from inside.

Tell us where you've been and what you did with uncle, Jimmy, sweetie, Teri whispered. She pulled the girl closer into her body.

As Timpany told the story it became obvious she thought Uncle Jimmy (whoever that was) had taken her on a vacation with our consent. She was fed and unmolested, except the finger.

Mommy, I'm hungry. Teri was so happy her girl had an appetite after this ordeal she jumped to the kitchen to make food.

I made salad! Your favorite! She grabbed the tongs.

No no, I want eggs and sausage. I can cook it myself, Uncle Jimmy showed me.

Okay, my big girl, Teri said. I could see she was starting to lose control. Tears were forming. I know we have eggs and I think I saw a sausage link in a Tupperware, she continued. I looked up. Teri tucked the tongs under her arm pit. The blood rushed out of my face. Teri reached past the bowl of crisp greens and grabbed the Tupperware. Here it is! Her fingers pinched the plastic lid. As she opened it a tiny foul smelling belch of air escaped. My god! she screamed. The tongs dropped to the tile [clank clank]. The smell was like shit. Teri jerked and the rotten finger sausage came flying out of the Tupperware like a bat out of a nightmare and landed in Timpany's lap.

Oooooggggg! she screamed and flapped the rotten zombie finger sausage bat off of her like she was covered with red ants. The finger landed on the floor. It pointed right at me. Teri looked at me like it was a roach I should step on. Timpany and her mother backed up to the farthest perimeter away from the dead digit. Teri lifted Timpany into her arms and held tight.

Ted, what is going on here? Teri demanded.

I… uh, I. I can't explain.

Ted! She said with a stern finality that frightened Timpany who whimpered.

Okay, okay. I let out a heavy sigh. We stood on opposite sides of the kitchen with the finger between us. I was at work. Driving the cart. Doing tickets for expired meters along Fifth Avenue. This crazy looking punk comes out and he's got his middle finger shoved in my face. He was chanting Meterpigs must die! Meterpigs must die! And I lost my cool. I hit him. I think I clipped his shoulder. He came at me. My hands went to choke him, we wrestled and… [sigh] I must have bit off his finger. Teri had her hand in her mouth biting on a finger nail, horror-struck. I don't remember. It all happened fast.

You didn't tell the police when Timpany was missing? she said. My head hung low with shame.

Timpany pulled her head away from her mother's breast. She pushed away a strand of hair, wet with tears, that was sticking to her face. I wasn't missing Mommy, I was with uncle Jimmy. He took me to Disneyland and taught me how to ride a bike. Teri started crying.

I didn't know, I mean, at first, I didn't want to lose my job and—uh—you, uh said if I got in any more fights you were gonna leave me—and uh, I didn't have enough info about the guy to help the cops.

Not enough info! You had the man's finger! She pointed at the rotting corpse on the floor. You stupid, ugggh, son-of-a-bitch! Teri shouted through heaving sobs. Timpany's own tears rekindled and she too choked and sputtered in sync with her parents' fear.

I thought you threw it away when you cleaned out the fridge... Ted went on. The argument got smaller and smaller becoming a microdot as we leave the scene. We reach the clouds, pass the moon, wave good-bye to the solar system and reach for the stars.

# SHAWN NELSON

It's one of those time frames where there's a news buzz in the air. Wherever you are you feel it and you remember where you were because of what happened. This feeling is associated with big wrenches in the machinery. A world leader is shot, a holocaust uncovered, a war ignited, a terrorist attack. For me, it's the little wrench cast in by the little guy, the real guy, that makes the impression. If you live outside my county, this event didn't touch you, though it was all over the network news. Nevertheless, it affected me. I was in a cafe, drinking my coffee black as usual. Bart was there, telling me about the script he'd pitched to some independent filmmaker about Hitler mowing the Rabbi's lawn in hell.

A National Guard tank rolling through the neighborhood where I used to live, smashing cars, rolling over street signs. A burgeoning chaos unfolding onto the freeway, the cops rendered helpless. A trail of busted white picket fence slats, a fire hydrant geyser. A plume of black smoke. Cop cars can follow tanks, but that's it. SWAT rifles don't penetrate military steel. Better get some vigilante gangbangin' drug dealers down here with real weapons. In case you missed it, here's the headline: TANK DESTROYS SUBURB. I'm intrigued because it's absurd. The guy hot-wired a tank. A televised pursuit followed until the hijacker tried to lose the cops by driving over the concrete Jersey barrier and got hung up. One of the treads shook off like a limp sock. He was left teetering, helpless like the suburbanites who watched their material crap get smashed flat. Didn't matter by that time because the news copter was on the scene. A gung ho ex-Marine cop leaped onto the tank, snapped the lock with a bolt cutter, and fired his police issue .38 down the hole. Not so much as, Come out with your hands up.

I said before this influenced me. The tanks had been sitting in the National Guard Armory for years down the street from a house I rented. I imagined myself going for a cruise, but never seriously imagined I could get in, start 'er up, and roll. That's the difference between a guy like Shawn Nelson and me. Didn't take long for the news to report the guy being dragged lifeless and bloody from the disabled tank was Shawn Nelson, resident loner of the neighborhood where the tank was stolen. He did it. Of course, the news tried to paint him as a crazy, they snooped around in his drawers and found his porno mags and stuff like that. He had also been digging a deep hole in his backyard. About that, we can only speculate. A few days later it wasn't news and they were on to something else.

When I walk the streets I imagine I'm a wanderer roaming America. I think maybe I'll keep walking on my pilgrimage to the end of time. Today I thought maybe I could do it, pretty face credit card begging meals from restaurants and accepting an offer to share a sandwich from a pretty girl. I was walking north this morning, a foggy gray overcast day hanging over but not invading me. I was in a downtown area, under the shadow of tall buildings I have no reason to enter. Don't know who works or lives in these giant toy blocks of commerce. Earlier I watched a parking enforcement officer chalking tires on Fifth Avenue—chalk and cruise, chalk and cruise. Her funny electric cart reminds me of a clown car, except it's painted like a police state. Ever ask a meter maid why he picked the job? I think they're trained to answer, You're the one breaking the law buddy! Hey relax, it's not my car. I was wondering what possesses someone to specialize in bumming people out. They never answer, just move on like got a mission.

I spent the morning talking to Lilly who owns a bookshop on Fifth. She hates parking enforcement officers too. Thinks the dearth of customers downtown emanates, in part, from fear of parking tickets. She got a new shipment: Death Scenes, Garbage People, Severed, Deviant. They specialize in serial killers. We share small talk, no gossip worth repeating.

Around one o'clock I decided to walk on. Nothin' to do no place to go but north. Shawn Nelson was headed north in that tank when he cracked up. I stop for a slice of pizza, sign said ¢.99 but the clerk asked me for a buck zero seven. I hope they don't spend my tax money on more tanks. The gray sky is moving in on me. The chill crawls through my flannel, twangs my ears through the black watchcap. My scars itch. The pizza's not great, it's been under a heat lamp. All kinds of crazies out here trying to get away without working. Like me. That one dude in the sailor shirt, sailor cap, and bell bottom trousers is looking ratty. His hair coming out like Bozo. He's been wearing that same outfit for years, which is too small now. The big man who pees on himself in front of the public library is out today too. He hasn't got a shirt. His hair is going up like smoke from the burning building in his brain. He doesn't bother to panhandle, like the lady with no teeth, hand in my personal space.

Sorry, I mutter.

No sweat Birdman, she says. Why call me Birdman? Who knows? No one knows. Looks like rain. The cops are going to crack down on panhandlers and squatters by writing citations. Fined for having no money. Hey man, can you spare a dollar? I got vagged and wanna pay this beggar citation fore they lock me up.

I got a room about a mile outside downtown under the flight path on Union. The planes roar in at all hours. Rent's cheap. It's not a bad neighborhood. Mostly immigrants, families, young white couples lacking dough who think it's cool. The gangbangers call themselves the Woptown Krazy

Boys. I saw them writing on the wall once but they ran off like I cared. I mean, I do care, I wish they'd write something more interesting than their names, but paint isn't easy to steal. And who's got time for vertical manifestos? Commodities are the opium of the people. Before I get out of the downtown, I count the parking meters. Sometimes I put nickels in the expired ones, but here on the outskirts, all the meters take quarters. Time is money sayeth the law. Shoot. The Parking Insurrection Guard has got a VW bug in her mandibles. She has stepped out of the cart to get the goods on the license plate. There's a peace sticker on the window. The electric cart is about two car lengths north of the scene of the crime. As I walk by I hear the motor running. I look at her. She's busy. I look at the cart. It's automatic. Gas pedal, e-brake, not so complex. I think of Shawn Nelson. News said he had experience driving a tank in Germany for the army. She's walking south to give the next car a ticket. Did I throw away those porno mags Cecil Gonococci gave me or leave them in the drawer?

# PISSING RHINO

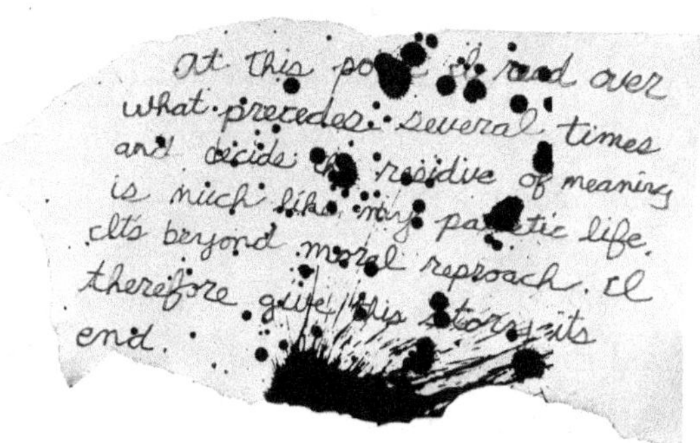

I find incredible things on First Avenue near the Bay View Medical Center. I found a dildo. I found a flyer promoting white supremacy, attacking immigrants: White Men Built this Nation. Ha ha ha. What a load of crap. Have these guys heard of slavery? The railroads dug out by the Chinese? Food supplied by migrant labor? Poor people built this country. Then there was the photocopied picture of the dead woman. Hundreds were strewn in the wind. I showed the picture to a cop and he said the lady was asleep. There was no life in her granite skin and her bare tits sagged with a heaviness like death. It was here that I found "The Suicide Note," not photocopied but original, unsigned and flecked with what I assumed to be blood. The top half was torn away. It could have been a sick hoax. The cultural production of a litter artist. Who knows? Today while my wife harped on me about getting a job, so our family could move to a better neighborhood, I thought about the note. And when she walked out the door, To get away, I took the note out and read it. And when she called and said, I'm not coming back until you get a job, I didn't know what to do, so I wrote this story about a rhinoceros.[1]

I was at the zoo with my daughter, Ariadne.[2] She'd turned nine and said things like Andy's mom's pregnant? I didn't even know she had sex. Andy's her cousin. My daughter and I have been hanging out because her mom works and I don't. And we took Ariadne out of school because her third-grade teacher delighted in grinding children's self-esteem with the pestle of her wit in the mortar of her own frustrated life.[3]

So I take Ariadne to the zoo and we study animals. We watch their behavior, covering two enclosures per visit. Earlier today we investigated the black rhino. d. Bicornis. The first thing about this mammoth pachyderm was that it isn't black. Its skin was more like gray than black, but more like black than white. I heard the white rhinoceros isn't white either. It's more like gray than white, but more like white than black. The zoo has one male and one female black rhi-

---

[1] Unreliable Narrator.

[2] Girl's name or Greek myth? Is he Minos?

[3] Could teacher be the Minotaur?

no. The female was off exhibit, being pregnant, her insemination an example of the zoo's captive breeding program— though the last one resulted, sadly, in miscarriage. Ariadne studied daddy rhino as he munched grass from a metal trough. Rhinos chew like cows, she noted. Although I'm forthright with her, I don't say there are stupid humans in the world who kill rhinos in order to make magic powder out of their horns. Perhaps I missed a teachable moment. But when she asked Why? I'd have to explain impotence and that dicks stop working right at about age 30. And she might ask What's a dick? and we aren't ready for that because she's nine remember. So we spend a few minutes looking at the horn, contemplating its danger, noting how it divides the skull. One black eye focused on Ariadne, the other watched for news from the zookeeper about his expected family.[4] In between munching the rhino paced the dusty cage like a nervous father in a maternity waiting room, stopping, as I did nine years past, for a drink from a fifty-gallon drum.[5]

Eventually, the pressure weighed on his bladder. Watching the animals urinate and defecate is one of our favorite parts of a zoo trip. We stood in line for thirty minutes to see the Panda and when we got to the viewing area the female panda visible through the bamboo forest of her enclosure took a

---

[4] Speculation.

[5] Projection.

big crap. I offered light applause. When an elephant pisses, a trap door opens between its legs and gallons of water drop. We haven't seen the giraffe piss or the polar bear or the alligator. The queen of naked mole rats pisses on the food stores to render the females infertile and thus enslave them. We could wait our whole lives to see the slow loris piss, though I'd imagine he never makes it to the toilet.[6]

We attended the coronation of urinations the day the rhino pissed.[7] Straight back, parallel to his body. The urine sprayed fifteen feet with fire hose force. I was glad the rhino's ass was pointed at the back fence of his cell rather than at us, however, the little brown sparrow didn't share our enthusiasm.[8] The jet stream of rhino piss blasted the bird off the fence. Laughter, guffaw even, exploded from Ariadne's belly. I chortled with disbelief and amaze. We couldn't stop laughing. We laughed and laughed, probably to the dismay of the bird which was knocked to the ground, shaken, and left to preen its feathers, I think humiliated. The rhino failed to see the humor in his marksmanship, obviously, having more important things on his mind.

The incredible pissing rhino incident was funnier than when President Bush puked into the lap of the Japanese Prime Minister. It beat the time our kitten pooped in my

---

[6] A testable hypothesis

[7] Hyperbole.

[8] Anthropomorphism.

shoe. It beat the time when I took our kitten's picture with a sign around his head reading: I'm an asshole. It was funnier than the photograph I took of my daughter's first poop in the toilet (it may not be as funny as when I will show that poop to her first boyfriend). When I tell the rhino anecdote, it gets more laughs than when Roddy Flesh questioned my punk rock credentials because I bought a Ramones shirt at Hot Topic. He's not a real punk. Well, la de da. Helga Kropotkin (notorious anarchist and MFA poet who once said, A pie in every fascist face) suggested I shave my head into a fan mohawk and dye it blue at the salon.[9] Which I did. She added, Akkkkk. Here's a wad a street cred! Pttu. The gob arced like a meteorite entering my atmosphere. I could have dodged it, but dipped my head and caught it with the fan of my new blue mohawk, where, eventually, it dried and hardened into a crust. We both laughed so hard we wet our fashionable bondage gear. But I'm ahead of myself.[10]

Comic relief saves lives.[11]

Daddy, I miss my friends at school, Ariadne said one morning as we were going over the multiplication table. But I don't miss school. A jet rolled in for landing, punctuating her sentiment with thunder. The third-grade tyrant, Ms.

---

[9] Could she be the sidekick, mentor, hero? Theseus?

[10] Foreshadowing.

[11] Breaking the Fourth Wall

Diceros, taught Ariadne and I hard knocks, adding incalculable stress to our lives. I had had a nervous breakdown about a year before and hadn't been working. No real job meaning no real money meaning odd jobs for minimum wage meaning make rent and rice for dinner. It also meant no new clothes honey, no Disneyland kiddo, no buying a house dear. It meant sticking with the junker, even though a safer car might be prudent, which in the context of our family meant stress. But somehow lesser than both school and work stress.

I hate our life, Ariadne's mother said as we lied in bed. Her tone made me tiny, helpless, insignificant. She could kill a man with tone.

The system is broken if it allows teachers like Ms. Diceros to fuck up our kids, I said listlessly, with feigned sleep in my voice so I could get out of the conversation if it turned to my getting a job.

I was so angry when she said, Ariadne, you should be quiet, you can't even spell in front of the whole class. My teacher did the same thing to me.

Remember at open house when that crazy woman posing as an elementary school teacher said to us, I don't think Ariadne likes me. Our daughter clams up in her presence trying to protect the soft gelatinous center which more metaphysical types, like her mother, might call soul. It doesn't take a genius to discern her feelings.

She doesn't like you, she's afraid of you.

Then I won't talk to her at all, Diceros said. Turning to Ariadne, That hurts my feelings. It hurt her feelings? Can you believe that? Ariadne stared at her shoes, counting the eyelets, trying to shrink and disappear. Her lip quivered. Well, if she doesn't want to be here she can sit with the second-grade teacher or in the Special Ed room.

My fingers locked on the back of a student chair. I was shaking. I wanted to throw it across the room. I wanted to break the wall. I was about to tell the teacher to piss off into a lower depth of hell when Ariadne said, Daddy, we don't solve problems with violence. Her mother and I had said this to our daughter many times and in that tense moment, she said it to me. We had asked her to Use her words a dozen times, but my own words were about to fail. Her soft touch on my hand expelled the tension in my grip. I looked down into her eyes and she looked straight up into mine.

What kind of teacher mindfucks her class with statements like, Did you hear the news? An elementary school teacher brought a gun to class and shot three kids...

I went to the local Thrifty drugstore to buy Ariadne a pistachio ice cream cone. On my way out I put a super-soaker squirt gun under my black trench coat.[12] Shoplifting from heartless corporations is in line with the revaluation of my values, which reminded me of The Suicide Note when the guy said he was "beyond moral reproach." That line connected me with whoever wrote it. It didn't matter if I lived in a dumpy house or if some clown thought I wasn't punk enough. I don't think I would ever commit suicide like the guy in the note probably did, but like him, I could try to live "beyond moral reproach."

Needless to say, I went home and pissed in the super-soaker. A twelve-pack of amber ale facilitated the process though I got so pished my aim got faulty and piss splattered on the bathroom floor—so I stumbled into the kitchen, grabbed the sponge off the sink, got on my knees, thought about praying, for sanity, but remembered the gods themselves are insane. The sponge soaked up the errant urine. I squeezed every drop of my elixir into the squirt gun. The next day I went back to the store and shoplifted another. I stayed drunk for several days, made several trips to the store, bought several ice cream cones. Stowing all of my liquid waste in the super-soakers. I knew the bender was over when I couldn't get drunk. Ariadne's mother got fed up and moved home with her parents taking Ariadne. I slept until noon, gathered my yellow and pink artillery, and went to my daughter's former school.

---

[12] Gathering the weapons.

I picked up Helga because I needed someone who wouldn't be recognized. And who's more anonymous than a poet?

Helga and I discussed the mission and went to the school. She was wearing a flowered summer dress and Doc Marten boots. Her long hair fell across her shoulder. We parked the car across the street. The school bell rang and the children flooded out of the school like piss out of a rhino's ass. I pointed out a few third-grade boys and girls. I didn't feel bad about using them as pawns, since children this age can be nasty.[13] Tapping the nasty energy of children is what teachers do best, though they usually sick them on each other. Jenny is gifted; Billy is special.

If you guessed the girls and boys are going to soak the wicked teacher with the urine guns, you've guessed correctly. Helga gave a squirt gun to several girls and boys and explained what they would have to do if they wanted to keep them, leaving out the part about them being filled with stale urine. Helga was great at talking to children; she seemed to have a knack.

OK, here's what you have to do...

The kids took to task without restraint or second thought. They ran banzai screaming Rambo attack.[14] From my van-

---

[13] Gross generalization.

[14] Pop culture reference. Rambo dir. Kotcheff 1982.

tage, I saw them come up on the teacher, with the quickness of a spring sprung. The cynical Ms. Diceros made a melodramatic gesture of fright and the moment her mouth fell open the first girl opened the jet stream of piss from the pink and yellow plastic gun. Suzi was hollering, mouth agape, head jutting in slow-motion side-to-side like the gesture for NOOOO! but letting loose with Huzzah leaping out of her own tortured psyche. I could hear the liquid plash against Diceros's cheek. The rush of golden piss showered over her teeth, splashed on her tongue, and trickled down her esophagus into her stomach into the bloodstream to mingle with kindred thoughts in her polluted mind. Within the instant another boy opened fire with the water gun, assaulting her clothing, her hair, which many students believed to be a wig, bombarding her with an ocean of sterile alcoholic piss.[15] The young suppliants drew from memory every humiliation of every student in their class. For David who you ignore because he can't read. For Tina who you screamed at. For run another lap Brad you're getting fat. For Jesus who sits in the corner because he smells.

Unlike the rhino, the mad grimace of killers distorted their nine-year-old faces. A battle cry rose from tiny voice boxes, as the plucky whippersnaps laughed and whooped in harmony with the gurgling squawk from their teacher… and in a long moment, it was over. A deep sense of justice and

---

[15] Oxymoron.

relief fell over the kids as the teacher collapsed to the sidewalk like a house of shit in the rain. The urine ran in a sheet over her lips. She twitched on the ground. Something in her brain snapped and she tore at her urine-drenched frock ripping it to shreds, exposing two long stretch-marked breasts twisted like clownish balloon animals. She burped a little puke which gurgled out of her mouth and started to choke on it. The next hiccough brought vomit like a geyser. The backsplash of puke on her face caused her to spasmodically shit and piss herself. Her body quivered with shock, fear, guilt, and collapse. Did she faint? Was it a heart attack? Is she dead? She looks dead. Someone should call 911.

Helga was already in the car. I walked up to my daughter's former teacher. Her eyes were shut, her mouth hung open. The smell of the urine, vomit, and fæces repulsed me. Her skin was stone gray, like rhino hide, but she was more like a small bird on a split-rail fence stripped of dignity by an act of cosmic indifference.[16] Her chest was rising, falling, so she wasn't dead. Do you need a hand? She didn't answer though her eyes clicked opened. I picked up her coat, laid it across her body. She looked a lot like the dead woman in the photograph, which I kept as a memorial.

What's the matter? Helga asked as I buckled my seatbelt. Don't feel vindicated?

---

[16] Freudian slip? Did he mean cosmic justice?

It wasn't as funny as I thought.

Ya, well. Revenge isn't supposed to be funny.



It wasn't as funny as I thought.

Ya, well. Revenge isn't supposed to be funny.

64

## LONELY PLANET BOY

He orbits the sun in a cave on his asteroid dark and barren. The temperature remains below freezing. When it's this cold everything slows. Nights like this he'd sit in the shower and let the rain run over his gangly fetal-tucked torso until the landlord complained he used too much water. He didn't care about the landlord, but there was a sublime glade of old oak forest tucked into a crevice in his mind, which he called his dark green sensibility. It was the source of the doom he felt when he didn't recycle everything he consumed. He composted food scraps, he took the aluminum and steel cans, plastic and glass bottles, mixed and news paper to the recycling, but there was always a wrapper or tissue he didn't know what to do with. He stuffed these bits into a sack in the corner of his room. The recyclers wouldn't take used pizza boxes, so Riddley stopped ordering pizza. He didn't like going to restaurants, so in effect, he quit pizza. Which sucked. He could have lived on pizza, alone in his room. He wanted to be left alone. Mostly. Since his girlfriend left. But he also longed to be held. There was the pounding in his head. This stupid line from a song repeating in his mind, *There's no girls that want to touch me.* He didn't know why. Clyde, his partner in freelance pest extermination, said Riddley was a queer and should go to the bathhouse, that long anonymous building, to get a blow job.

Riddley grabbed the earworm and played it fast-forward in his head—

NoGirlsWannaTouchMeNoGirlsWannaTouchMeNoGirls

and slow—

Thharrs Noooo Girrrrllsss Waaahnaaa Ttttuhhhchhh Meeee—

He visualized each phoneme of each syllable of each word breaking into tiny pieces. The song stopped repeating; he crushed the earworm under the boot heel of his will. But an alphabet soup of broken letters orbited his skull like a shimmering ring of Saturn.

After sitting a little longer he realized the pounding was on the door. He sat still. Down in his underwear, his dick was hard. What was I thinking about? Why is my dick hard? Something in a dream forgotten. The knocking stopped. He went to the window and parted the mini-blinds with two fingers. Dust the mini-blinds, he said to himself. Peering out at the street, a cete of Adventists or Witnesses, he was never sure, met in colloquy on the corner plotting their next move. He supposed they were Mexican because when he'd opened to them in the past they spoke Spanish. They came around once a month like the landlord, though unlike the landlord, who wanted rent, he never understood what they were after. He pictured himself on the corner, in a wool suit, midsummer, holding a bible. He chuckled aloud. He fantasized answering the door naked, but they were neighbors and he'd never be rude to a neighbor. Sometimes he'd watch the mother and youngest daughter walk to school. Eyes on the street make a safe street. He liked to take his dick out and picture sexual positions with the Adventists. They prefer the Missionary, he thought chuckling to himself. One, in particular, was about four-foot-five. He thought maybe she was an aunt or older sister. Her skin looked supple and delicate, yet she was plagued with horrible acne. He liked the way her fingers dug into the leather of her bible; he gestured for it, flipped the pages, and dropped it into a burning bush. He placed his hand in hers. She wore a dark-colored dress appropriate for church, which was so well-made it was difficult, even in his imagination, to tear it off her body. After some effort, there she was, naked. His eyes inched across her skin like snails. She covered her breasts with both arms, at first, shivering more from fear than cold. Her nipples looked like wine. She clamped her gorgeous squat legs shut like she had to pee. When he reached for the bone hairpin that held her long black strands in a tight bun, she darted away. The hair released like a parachute, canopy-ing over her shoulders to tickle the top of her breasts. As she backed into the corner and raised her fists to a fighting pose, her breasts dropped, bounced, and came to rest.

Riddley got a rope from the kitchen drawer, which even here in his mind smelled of roach powder. He didn't want to hurt her, not even her feelings, nor was he ready to let go. She slapped him twice causing his head to jolt in this world, side to side with the percussive sting of sharp dual blows; he smiled. I have scars you can't touch, he said to her in his mind. The sting radiated from his cheek steeling everything on its way to the lower extremities. He tasted blood in the corner of his mouth.

I have to tie you up, he said wishing he'd watched a How To. Sorry if my clumsy knots are a great disappointment, he added as he wound the thick rope between her legs, bifurcating the lips and tightly looping the breasts, which were full and ripe like the fatted mammaries of a mature woman on the way to securing her wrists and ankles.

She reminded him of this girl he'd found passed out at a party who he contemplated feeling up. He'd unbuttoned her shirt, living in his mind even then, and licked the breasts, which had a nasty, stale taste of sweat that shocked him out of the reverie. As he stood up thinking, Better find her people. It's not safe being passed out with these jocks around, the girl's boyfriend stumbled through the door. Riddley remembered, although it too was like recalling a dream in the morning, being dragged by the hair, being kicked by a dray of muscle-headed jocks. He recalled being punched and broken at the wheel of their fists.

He left the Adventist or Witness tied up like that in the back of his mind. She shrunk from life-size to a microdot, falling through the cyberspace of his brain, until she became microscopic, the last point of light on a shut down monitor, microfiche … all he had to look forward to was another Saturday night surfing the internet for free porn thumbnail galleries.

## DRUG TESTING

The urine sloshed around in the plastic jar. The lid was screwed on tight. There wasn't enough pee in there so the man added water, just a little, went to the store for Perrier to be sure. Purity was essential. A few days later the lab called.

Hello Mr. Lee.

Yes, this is Jeff Lee.

Mr. Lee, Southwest Labs is happy to tell you you tested negative for drugs—

That's great!

Mr. Lee.

Yes?

You tested negative for drugs, but we're afraid… you're pregnant.

Mr. Lee felt stress about getting a higher paying job. He had been making decent money hacking computers at a small company. His rent was paid but he wanted to invest in comic books. His favorites were The X-Men and The Avengers and The Defenders. Oh and The Fantastic Four. He had a fiancé, who was Mexican-American, which was of no consequence to him but bothered his parents. His mom said the girl was too scrawny, but he knew her real objection. His fiancé was intelligent, self-sufficient, which was enough. He worried she was crazy, but that could be entertaining. When he looked in the mirror he saw a dumpy guy, which was hard to admit, since he'd fancied himself a good looking chap. He decided, No, I'm still good looking, it's stress. He needed to relax. He needed to get high. His mom still told people he'd been photogenic as a baby—funny how the meaning of that statement changes over time. By adolescence, he admitted he'd never be a movie star. That was hard. He found solace in the idea he was honest with himself. The hot job opportunity looked like his CV posted by mistake. College grad, computer programming, twenty-four to thirty. Must love money. The starting wage would be more than he'd ever imagined making.

Jeff had never smoked pot in high school. The kids he played Dungeons & Dragons with on Friday nights didn't smoke, so he didn't. His friends thought he was on drugs, sometimes, the way he played. His characters were always extreme. Always demented. They raped, murdered, plundered. His humans drank botas of wine in a gulp. His elves copulated with dwarves, his dwarves with hobbits. He felt comfortable on the ethereal plane or maybe it was cathartic.

As his parents got more affluent they pushed Jeff harder to emulate successful people. He came to associate happiness with money. But when he got to college being successful took work. You had to study. But if you studied all the time, you'd be keyed up and choke the exams. The successful people seemed to be smoking a lot of marijuana. So Jeff started smoking to relieve stress and since he created and carried gargantuan amounts, it would be fair to say he smoked a lot of dope.

When he found out he was hired for the new job, he was so excited and so confident he gave two weeks' notice to his soon-to-be-former boss. He figured he'd take vacation time to get prepped for the new position. Then he found out about the drug test.

 Before you start work you need to pass a drug test Mr. Lee.

Okay, I'll come in next week.

Fine. He put himself on a radical fasting diet. He drank gallons of water. He tried goldenseal to clean his system. His wetware was polluted, tainted by a virus. If they did a hair follicle test, he'd be toast. When the week rolled around, he called the lab and told them he was sick. Mr. Lee made another appointment and dodged that one. He was afraid the marijuana wasn't out of his system. Finally, the company who had almost-except-for this-minor-drug-test-formality hired him called wondering why he wasn't ready to come to work. He pissed in the jar they gave him. His urine was close to the color of water. To be sure he went to the store, bought a bottle of Perrier… you've heard this. He turned over his urine to the authorities. He thought about how much power he had given these lab workers, how strangers controlled his destiny.

His girlfriend believed she had power over him too. Their main trouble was in the bedroom. She used to say one of her psychoses manifested itself as sex addiction. Some guys thought living with a nympho would be heaven on earth heaven in the bedroom in the bathroom in cars in the dark at movies in parking garages, but he felt too much pressure. He didn't think he performed badly, but she gave him the sense something was lacking. Like when she suggested he put the new sex toy in her butt. Jeffy… move it lower lower… mmm… push it in. For a while she had brought all sorts of food to bed, smearing it on her body, Come on Jeffy… lick it. But he wasn't hungry. Instead of a turn-on, this was another thing to worry about. Is my penis inadequate? Is my attention to the details of the clitoral bump between her labia minora insufficient? He double-checked his calculations, but couldn't figure the formula to her climax? She asked if she could bring another woman to bed. He knew she'd dated women. If monogamy was a difficult equation, polyandry was a Poincaré conjecture.

He was sure, however, the new job would solve their real problem. His girlfriend didn't know he was in debt. She didn't know about the storage facility filled with comic books. Of course, his debt was her debt. His car was about to be repossessed, the rent was due, the credit cards were maxed. He looked in the mirror, he looked over at his girl-friend writhing on the bed like a wild naked hungry animal and the only thing he could think was that it was the mon-ey. She wants money. So she got less sexual attention and in turn, she nagged him about things she had never cared about before. Jeffy, I want to paint the bathroom pink. Jeff, can we take down the Wolverine™ poster?

Sunday morning, like every Sunday morning, Jeff Lee's par-ents called to ask, Where are our grandchildren to dote on? A week had gone by and still no word from the lab or the new job that would set all the miscreant tumblers in his life to sync. The job. The job. He saw the bong sitting on the end table in the bedroom. He still had a bag of weed wait-ing to provide relief to his anxiety. He loaded it, fired it up, and inhaled. He went to the ethereal plane. The next day the lab called. We're sorry Mr. Lee, we were not able to read your urine test, it was too watery. You'll have to bring an-other sample today.

Wow.

He smoked his future. He was like a Just Say No commer-cial. Demolition Man. His girlfriend jumped from bed making a beeline for the bathroom and he had an idea. He burst in on her and thrust a Cyclops Slurpee™ cup at her. Honey, pee in this cup. She smiled misinterpreting his request as the kink she had longed for. She'd read about water sports, golden showers. The hot urine swirled into the cup filling it halfway. She watched him take the cup to the sink and add an ounce of tap water. She got on her knees, eyes locked on the plastic cup, and started to unbuckle his pants, but he said, I've got no time for that. I have to take this pee down to the lab.

When she told her friends he was using her pee for the drug test, they all cracked the same joke. You tested negative for drugs, but we're afraid… you're pregnant.

She laughed with them but thought If he is, I am. Motherhood would be amazing. But she knew they had nothing to worry about. They hadn't had sex since he started chasing this new job. I don't think it's ethical, one of her friends said. She hadn't thought about it. For a second she considered calling the lab. As a woman though, as a lover, she felt it was her duty to give up her pee for her man. Her pee was their pee after all. She was making an investment and if Mr. Lee didn't lose the Wolverine poster above the bed, she could hold this over him.

I don't think drug testing is ethical, she said to her friend.

The funny part was Mr. Lee's test came back okay, he got the job, smoked dope with his new colleagues and probably designed part of your personal computer.

## fæces

Alaska asked me to bring her a stick of incense, which we had brought from the old country, the city where Mexican families used to mill around Pedro's vegetable truck, where queer white males sold off man-sized come-fuck-me pumps at garage sales, and where a jet roared in low overhead for landing every three to five minutes. This new suburban apartment, the place we moved to, is kind of like living in a hospital, except instead of pushing us toward wellness it makes us sick. I touched a lit match to the stick and a plume of strawberry smoke meandered to my nostril like a pleasant ammonia. It reminded me of the love we used to have in our downtown flat. The burning ember of the incense was the core of our love. Over the trailing fruity effusion, I could smell a faint methane. I stepped into the bathroom suppressing a sour face. Alaska's black jeans were gathered at her ankles and the triangle of pubic hair between her thighs was like the welcome mat I'd wiped my feet on a thousand times. A black lace bra covered her breasts, though a pink whisper of nipple peeked from one cup.

I set the incense in its wooden scabbard to collect the gray ash before it sullied the floor tile. I unsnapped my trousers, let down the zipper. My penis floundered out, as noiselessly as any snake slithering through any grass. Alaska accepted the head into her mouth perched on the toilet, sucking like taking a drag on a cigarette. It was all I could do to contain myself. She exhaled through puckered lips, blowing not swift enough to whistle. The air reacted with her saliva sending a cool wave from synapse to synapse. We are quiet when it comes to acts of sex. We learned sex with parents sleeping in other rooms or under the laugh track of a roommate's TV show. Even though we'd been living together for years we fucked as quiet as church mice. (I am certain I've never heard mice fuck in church.)

It was so quiet in the bathroom while Alaska inhaled my penis I could hear the long tube of shit pushing out of her ass, sliding into the toilet water. The shit took to the water slow, like a bather testing one foot, an ankle. It fell full body all at once—splash. The sound tuned my sense of smell like the dial of a radio. As soon as my brain realized (reified) the paradigm that was shifting, as soon as it recognized the happening as a happening and not just shit dropping into a toilet, I came. Alaska bit hard and pushed me away. A gob of white spume glopped on the floor. Glee. I looked down searching for her eyes tilting her chin with the tip of one finger. She giggled.

The next morning I had that regular pulling urge inside. The first rod of shit sprung out of my body like a javelin. It crashed into the toilet like a barge sinking. The spearhead dredged the bottom of the porcelain bowl before the bulk cleared my anus. I had to lift up off the warmed seat, so the train could continue. Here was this tremendous shit piled into the bowl so the tail end stuck smelly out of the water like the mast of a tall ship battered on the reef, yet I was unsatisfied. The rest of my shit would be a long time coming. I might have to wipe and go on with my day while the chamber reloaded. Years of practice and I don't know shit about my bowels.

Alaska bring me an incense, will you?

In a minute Jimmy, I'm on the phone.

That was a long minute. I was caught without a book to read, without a journal to write in. I didn't even I have an ink pen so I could write limericks on the inside of my boxer shorts. I whittled time by staring between my legs. My penis was shriveled leaving plenty of room to view the log languishing in the toilet. It had a thick body and a texture like clay. It was light brown with a tinge of yellow streaking back from the middle. The exposed tip created a disturbing effluvium. It was an uncomfortable contemplation and when it was over, I was left with the strange desire to reach into the bowl and squeeze the cylinder of shit and feel it ooze through my fingers.

At this moment Alaska walked in with a stick of nag champa. The dynamic of the smell in the room shifted slowly. Alaska turned to throw open the window. It was nothing like the shoe box window in our downtown bathroom where I watched the neighbors shave a dead pig, where the planes touched down on the runway for our amusement. Something in the angle of Alaska's nude shoulder blade struck me with a crazy desire. The black lace bra strap was the first bold brushstroke on my canvas. Alaska was primping to go out with Lulu Godardo. I leaped from my throne and unlatched the bra with a quick snap of two fingers.

No, don't turn around, I said planting a small kiss on her back, dragging up to nibble an ear and caress the shimmering red flag of her hair. My khaki-colored Dickies fell around my ankles as the belt buckle clanked sonorously against the tile. Alaska held the incense like a torch allowing the smoke to rise to be vacuumed out the window.

When Alaska unsnapped her own pants and dragged her "vibrator" (my right hand) to her pudendum, I reached my other hand into the cold water of the toilet. When my fingers clasped around the shit I was thrilled electric across my pores. The instant with my hand in the toilet amplified all the naughty things I'd ever done. Every hand-in-the-cookie-jar flashed in montage across my eyes. A sly grin filled my being. Everyone was watching. I could hear the in-laws gasp; I could see my mother hurl with revulsion; I could see Alaska's mother faint dead on the floor; my father's blood vessels burst at his temple raining a screaming rage of blood past his crow's feet spraying his gray…

The shit oozed through my fingers. I squ-ee-ee-zed and my diminutive cock vaulted forth. It was like holding a melted chocolate bar, like playing mud pies in the backyard 1969. I collected all the crap I could with one hand trapping it against the bottom of the bowl. Scooping. My right hand completing the circuit to Alaska's back so caressing her smooth skin. When my left hand broke the water's surface I was afraid she would notice the water running off to the toilet, so I spoke to camouflage intent.

Drop your pants for me honey, but don't turn around, I said. There was an air of something about to happen. The shit was warm in the palm of my hand. The shape of the log was gone. It was like holding a handful of human mud. Alaska's pants hit the floor and her beautiful buttocks rose like the moon. The black G-string accenting its delicate mass. I was shocked by the contrast between butt cheek and middle back. And it is not easy to shock a man standing with a handful of his own shit wavering above the toilet, eyes gleaming like a mad man. What would she think? How would she react? She might leave. She would scream. What could it mean if she liked it? What if she gushed onto the tile or balled like a human baby slapped insane by a freak prank loud crash of toys hurled off shelves breaking under the heel of earth's fury?

His evil fetishistic brain reeled mad questions across his mind frame like a slot machine coming up cherries. Jackpot! He smeared the warm mass of shit in a slow rolling wave starting between her shoulder blades, following her spine to the base of her ass. She arched forward in ecstasy and Jimmy could see her own fingers massaging. She gyrated against his palm which smeared and smoothed the balm of shit across her back. Slower than you'd think the shit smell overpowered the nag champa. There was a second when Jimmy thought the incense with the help of a vile waft of some neighbor's breakfast bacon riding an incoming wind would prevail, but the toxic shit stench bum rushed their nostrils.

Aaagghh! she shrieked.

Alaska was at first repulsed. She felt the urge to puke. Her stomach chewed its contents. Jimmy could see her sickened, yet his hand kept massaging the shit into her muscles. Yet, her hand kept digging and sh-huffling between her legs. They continued on the verge of sickness riding a wave of ecstatic nausea. His diminutive penis begged entry like a dog at the dinner table to which she consented by tilting her hips and leaning forward. As they fucked his fecal massage continued with a pulsating rhythm. The fæces spread like fire, wild across dry scrub hills and valleys. Soon his chest was smudged with earthy grafts of his own waste. The brown badge of excrement! He came whirling her around to catch a glimpse of thought in her eyes. He was so excited. It was the first time in a year her thoughts were a mystery. She looked deep into his sick mad eyes. The radiant blue so far from the hue of shit, yet so like the shit in oneness with it. Their embrace lasted uncountable minutes radiating passion.

The doorbell was ringing. It was Lulu Godardo.

Before the second ring Jimmy was in the shower naked. The patches of shit slipped off his body to ride the whirlpool around the drain. Jimmy hopped out of the shower into his boxer shorts and ran for the door while Alaska climbed in the shower. Jimmy answered the door laughing like a crazed buffoon. Godardo filled the doorway.

What's that smell?

Jimmy looked at her without answering. He hadn't had time to fully think through their lavatory escapades. He replayed the events in his mind in lieu of a response, allowing Lulu to speak.

Jimmy what's wrong? What's wrong with you? A patch of fecal matter remained on his shoulder.

Huh? He struggled to find speech. Nothing, he said. Alaska's taking a shower.

That's funny, I talked to her a few minutes ago and she said she already took a shower. There was an unsteady pause as Jimmy slid into his scatological reverie. Were you guys doing it when I rang? Having sex?

Uh. No. Uh. She was feeling dirty. You know how she gets when it's hot. He wasn't sure why he was lying. Jimmy had never had a problem talking about sex, especially with Lulu Godardo who was half voyeur and half carnal encyclopedia.

Jazz-man, relax. Hey Jimmy? she said. He was startled from his reeling phantasmagoria of dung. Hey, is your toilet backed up? Do you have some kind of plumbing issue? I've got a strong plunger in my car. Fuck. The smell reminds me of Pasolini's Salo: 120 Days of Sodom.

I haven't seen that one. Tell me about it, he said swimming against the riptide toward reality. Lulu sat on the white couch. She looked around the house with mild bewilderment.

The film concerned these bourgeois fascists in Italy who kidnapped Jewish children. There was sex, coprophagy, torture… it was disgustingly bizarre, but I liked it.

Coprophagy?

Alaska emerged from the shower. I'll be out in a second Lulu. A towel ran over her body. Another towel had been wrapped like a turban over her hair.

It's a kind of shit fetish.

You told her! Alaska exclaimed.

No. You just told her. Lulu looked puzzled, but sniffed the air.

Hey Alaska, what's that smell? Alaska turned on point, marching to the bathroom. Jimmy and Lulu heard the shower restart. There was a long awkward moment of silence. The sound of the raining water dulled as Alaska's body stepped under it.

Jimmy, what's going on with you two? You're acting weird.

You mean weird even for us? The phone rang. No one moved to pick it up. It rang again. Cecil's voice came on the answering machine. Jimmy picked up the handset. Alaska dressed in the bathroom. Lulu hovered outside the hollow door.

Hey girl, I have to go. Hurry up! Lulu called. Her voice slipped under the door like an unwelcome portent of doom. Alaska noted the brown streaks of shit on the bathroom wall, on the door, floor, sink and tub as if Jackson Pollack had been their house guest.

Alaska said, Use the other bathroom, through the bedroom.

Later that night Jimmy sat at the table while Alaska described lunch. Jimmy tried to intuit her feelings. He couldn't. He wanted to ask her what she thought about the experience. Alaska became afraid. She recognized her boyfriend's need to go beyond, to the outer limits, the drive to outdo what could not be undone. His sanity seemed to be locked up in shit.

They kissed. The first kiss faded into a long comfortable silence which in turn faded to passionate kisses. Soon they were naked and making love on the bed. Jimmy was prowling around like a jungle cat. He had energy Alaska hadn't seen since they moved from the city.

They wrestled and caressed. They laughed and kissed for hours. They screwed in different positions. Jimmy went down on her. She came twice, but he wouldn't stop his unrelenting oral attack. Finally she felt like she needed to shit.

Stop honey, I have to go to the bathroom.

That word "bathroom" hung in the mist of their sex like a demon, an omen. Jimmy pounced. Springing on the pink pastel down comforter. He grabbed her by the shoulders shaking her with unbridled joy.

I… have… an… idea.

Alaska froze struck with solemnity.

Baby, he said calmly. Let's clap our sphincters together. Alaska didn't understand but he spun her around and maneuvered his own body so their assholes connected in a tight kiss. When that pressing need to move bowels twinged inside her, she tried to break free, but Jimmy held tight. He looked at her through a tangle of limbs. He loved the way her body had evolved over the years, the way the muscles in her arms had changed from skinny girl arms to those of a strong woman. Once her eyes caught his in a furtive glance Alaska realized what needed to be done. Jimmy reached over to the night table, fumbling for the incense. He struck a match and watched a single sage-scented swirl rise to the ceiling.

## VAPID HOLES

I woke up with your pussy smell all over me. Sometimes, tick-tock, if I haven't showered in a while after a stressful sweaty day, I can generate my own pussy smell with the evidence gleaming on the length of one finger post wiping the crack in between my scrotal sack and top of the leg inner thigh. But it was your dank pungent wavering pussy smell (not mine) in my hair, up and down the length of my arms where you slid your fanatic clitoris, on the balls of both knees where you balled and humped and fucked. Your dehydrated pussy smell was heavy in the wrinkly skin of my fingers, knuckle to knuckle odoriferous, which I scrubbed and scrubbed and scrubbed in the shower with a hard brush. Somehow your rich pussy smell, like the smell of new soil or garlic worked its way into my pores.

While we were fucking, or should I say while you were fucking, (I was sort of laying stiff and amazed) I had to fart. It was one of those bubbly wet flatulent sea monsters that leave a stain. I held it with a technique I learned in the Navy, swallowing huge gulps of air so the fart is diluted or dispersed inside the intestines. That kind of breathing, even if it breaks rhythm, goes unnoticed in such sexual escapades. In the case of last night's sex ball, it was drowned by the grunts and thumps and moans emanating from your vagina. The lips opening and closing and sloshing and frothing may have been loud enough on their own to jam the senses, to drown the smell, to blot reality but I wasn't about to take that chance. I care about you that much. You looked happy, having a good time, and that kind of thing strokes my ego.

It's 10:30 and you've changed your outfit four times. This ritual is vanity, fashion show fantasy. Reptilian and puerile. I've never met a woman tall enough to be a runway model and don't care to. She parades and twirls each frock for my benefit or maybe because I'm plopped in the armchair next to the full-length mirror. I can jump into that fucking-the-magazine model fantasy as easily as I can criticize. Off the page into my own flop house shack abode, life-size three-dimensional mastur-friggin-bation, and when the cum slaps your face, I don't have to worry about the semen-stained paper getting withered. I don't have to clean the monitor. She asks each time how she looks. Each time I say, Smashing, looking good, sexy right on let's go splendid. Though I sometimes wonder how close the inverse—You look like shit in a pile of dirty cum rags—would take me to the edge of death.

The final outfit is a variation of the first and third. It's a hybrid. You like it so we have consensus. Out the door to the bar, which stinks like it always does—last night's and last month's and the last thirty years' sloshed beer evolving new yeasts in the cracked floor. This place is an ashtray with loud music. But the historically illiterate musicophants didn't come to hear music. They didn't come to drink. They couldn't hold a conversation for ten minutes about Snoopy. They spend their money on the wrong pinball machine in search of instant gratification. The machine complies with a ten-ball multiball, it bings, whizzes, flashes. You scored a million points. You are a winner it says, lying just like you to the drunk girls you bring home. It's a sad place full of stupid people. They came to be seen because somebody told them it was cool. Years from now when the radical thought-provoking poets and guitar heroes who wailed their gig to gig town to town lungs out for gas money and two free drinks win Nobel prizes, the huddled masses in this joint will say, I was there. Sure, you were there in the back bar by the bathroom where the light is ambient trying to look cool. I was there pushed against the stage, banging and shaking, drinking Irish whiskey and dancing and listening as deeply as I could to lyrics that blew my mind.

Sometimes when I lay down a heavy line of negative shit about the vapid holes of minor hipsterdom my good friend, the writer of this story will play Lucifer's advocate. Give them a break. Everybody has their own way. They paid to get in. They paid for you to see that band. But who is he kidding? Most of the people who pay for shit around here are stupid and posing. And when they go home, they leave their feigned alternative values swilling in the sour carpet.

No wonder it smells. Their desire to return to the work-week race to material satisfaction smells like the shit it is. When I walked away from the values of my father, I wasn't changing my outfit for a night on the town. I reconstructed my values so I can fuck whoever I please without shame. I can call for more the next day without any fear-of-intimacy cliché because I've spent years creating my own clichés. If the woman doesn't have anything intelligent to say, I tell her straight out I'm using her body for sex.

The last girl, Nadine, was twenty-three. She hadn't been to school passed the twelfth grade, but her ass was tiny and her tits were large and firm. Imagine large and firm. I told her the first night before I jammed a hot hand into her pussy, that I had reconstructed my values and that our relations were to be based on mutual pleasure. Luckily she was as horny as gridlock traffic and dove straight for the blow job. Whoa. I have never had my cock sucked so hard. She left a black bruise on the shank of my penis that would have made Sade gawk. Smooth operator hadn't read the Marquis; she couldn't read the cartoon bubbles in the funny papers, but she knew how to make pain feel good.

The first date killer blow job was her hook into a man. But she couldn't reel in her fish, couldn't scale, gut, fry nor slap him on a plate at the dinner table. I told her I loved her so she'd suck it again. I continued to like her best with my dick in her mouth, soon enough because I didn't have to listen to her talk.

Do you think it's worse to be a vapid hole minor hipster or just plain Joe-Blow-Jock in the hole average everyday football watching vapid? The real evil, the thing that bugs me, is when the bands cater to poseurs to sell records. They soften it, make it easy. They dumb it down. I hate that. Fucking poseur liberals are almost as bad as rockabilly Republicans. Pop culture is being spoon-fed to them by the radio, by MTV, by all the forces that hold them in awe. The message is for them. The call to action comes through with cable TV clarity! All you need to do is dangle your stupid chain wallet and adjust the straps on your tiny backpacks. You don't have to read Chomsky. You don't have to pay attention. You don't have to care about the environment. Buy some shit and shut up. Ok, so there is a lot of stuff I know nothing about. I undergo tremendous enterprises of foolishness and phase, I'll admit, to appear as cool and wise as the Greek philosopher So-crates who said he was the smartest guy because he knew zilch. I admit to separate myself from you. I think about the world.

She rolls over and pretends to be sleeping. The alarm clock catches her thinking about gathering her tackle box for a trip to the pond.

# THE EXAMINED LIFE

This morning Riddley Harroway was probably the least interesting person on Ivy but that was about to change. He lived in a "cozy" (read small) cottage next to a larger apartment complex which blocked the sun when it bothered to appear. He sometimes greeted the doddering lady in the brick house who fed pigeons on the corner, even though the accretion of guano her turtledoves had shat over the years struck him as a health menace. From his apartment he spied a young white male on the balcony of a 1920s plaster flat roof house drinking coffee staring at the harbor or the planes coming in. He never wondered about his neighbors, never wondered what they did for work or to what they aspired. It never struck him to care. He saw them though. The old man of the sea a few houses down rarely looked up from his nets in the driveway. The Mexican family on the cross street kept to themselves. Sometimes they had late-night parties with ranchera music ringing through their open kitchen door. There were a lot of stylish, he supposed, apartments on the block dating midcentury, so it was a matter of time before gentrification set in like rigor mortis. The city had planted date palms in the 40s, but they'd been cut, uprooted, and paved over for the crime of interfering with telephone wires. A vacant lot overrun with weeds offered the only vivid colors. Green in the spring but a goldenrod Van Gogh might envy by summer's end. Even the sky was gray most of the year, June Gloom they called it. A high-pressure system invading by sea. The general atmosphere of a barren-womb made Riddley think if he could live here, he could live on Mars. Most people would go crazy on Mars, he thought, without seeing blue when they looked up at the sky. Without trees or animals. With all that red. There are all kinds of animals in the city if you count the garbage eaters. Crows, rats, raccoons, possums, skunks, feral cats. The feral cats on his block seemed nervous, stalking around trashcans for scraps, mice, roaches. Maybe he projected that onto the poor creatures. Perhaps cautious would be better.

Riddley spent time collecting and reading books on anatomy. His parents, through the years, had bought dozens of lay-medical books for him, which never satiated his appetite. He guessed they couldn't understand the kind of expertise he craved. He was an autodidact after all but didn't blame them for that either.

Riddley liked to think of himself as a medical practitioner, amateur doctoring was more than a hobby. His day job was something more like janitor, even if it was in a hospital. He was responsible for sterilizing the operating room, a very important job, at the University Medical Center. He held the keys to many secrets, on one of those retracting key chains hooked to his belt. Access to the forefront of medical knowledge was his, though he avoided talking to the other doctors. Their power came from a degree on the wall. His from inspired genius. In six years of this employment. he had taken sly advantage of his position. Meticulously strewn about the powder blue wood-paneled cottage were trays of forceps, clamps, scalpels—the requisite tools. Everything a Sunday surgeon could want—his vintage Jack Nicholson clubs were three short of a set. Last week he was able to pilfer the last part for an electrocardiograph from the Receiving Department. The Medical Center officials were officially perplexed at the consistency of faulty machines that had come in the hospital in the last five years.

Enough parts have been left out by your company to build a unit! the chief administrator barked over the phone, unaware of the truth he'd uttered. Once, on a dusky afternoon in July, Riddley was questioned by Medical Center security while removing the hulls of two high-powered surgical lamps.

I'm going to use them in a sculpture, Riddley told him.

Wow, man. Art is like. Ya. I can dig it, the guard replied. He'd been a minor beat poet in his youth. His black turtleneck sweater, beret, and conga were packed in an iron-banded trunk in the attic with his mortgage and a volume of unpublished poetry. He re-adjusted the waistline of his khaki uniform and smiled.

That was the last time Riddley was questioned for carting away hospital castoffs. In the time since, he and the guard exchanged telling smiles three times, shared a gratuitous nod, and even winked.

The 1000-watt light bulbs Riddley procured gave an exact illumination to his kitchen/lab. The light played on the stovetop with a brilliance that demonstrated his janitorial prowess. The powerful light defied bacteria to dwell in its presence. The microscope left of the sink looked as natural there as any toaster or blender. The refrigerator kept six bags of type AB neg blood plasma cool. As the lone low-sodium street lamp crackled outside, Riddley grimaced over his six-hour supply of anesthesia. He tapped the tiny glass vials with his index nail. Would it be enough?

A Southwest Air 767 scraped the sky overhead. If it weren't for the planes Riddley might complain about the ever-present hum of the freeway.

He sat upright in the tub cleansing his abdomen with a stiff-bristled brush. He reflected on the day five plus years ago when he had been rereading Hamlet, pondering "the question." He liked to have the TV on in the background while he read to keep his thoughts from wandering too far. He recalled a mercurial voice shattering his rumination:

The answer is within you.

Riddley had leaped to his feet, the book fell into the water, pages fanned out like Ophelia's skinny arms, a chain reaction of ideas rebounding through his skull. In his excited rush to shut off the set he knocked the TV off its stand with a huge crash. Lacking the human capacity for sustained revelation the television "died" and the room fell dark.

As he watched the water drain from the tub, illuminated by the streetlight outside his window, Riddley laughed aloud. That had been the sign he'd been waiting for; it all made sense. "Thee Answer" was within his grasp. His readings, his job, his whole existence had been a preparation. The answer was like a vein of gold in a hillside waiting excavation. To grab a hold of it, own it, and savor enlightenment like… like his weakness for double-chocolate cheese cake. The precise manner with which he dried himself showed to the adequate observer a steady unshakable hand and to the insightful observer a streak of narcissism. The last swirl of water carried particles of dirt, drowned bacteria, and dead flakes of Riddley's skin screwing down the drain. He knew, as he had known the answer was within.

Staring into the naked luminescence of the surgical lights, Riddley was lost day-dreaming an out-of-body near-death experience. It was overwhelming and beautiful. As his eyes adjusted to the light, a leather strap near his right leg came into focus. It worked on him like a souvenir jogging a memory. Like the snow globe from the Grand Canyon he used to keep on his dresser. The stark realism of the thick black leather strap jolted him to the reality of the moment. He knew the task before him was absurd, but at this point he expected The Answer to be—Not to be. He tightened the strap. He put on the blue-paper doctor's mask and double-checked the fluid delivery monitor. He waited as another plane came in for landing. In theory, the anesthesia would render the major part of his body inert, leaving his brain, arms, and hands working with full coordination. He thought about a basic definition of Human—a mind with hands. He thought too about those who anesthetized themselves to hide from pain, like his neighbors whose trashcans clinked with empty alcohol bottles as they carted them to the curb on trash day. He didn't count himself among them.

The rubber gloves on his fingers altered his control over the needle. He felt between the ridges of his spine, pausing with the point breaking the skin on his back. The cold hard spike pierced the sixth thoracic vertebra; penetrating deeper it discharged its fluid into the white matter of the nerve cell. Riddley exhaled and shakily reached for the oxygen mask. Inhaling, he waited. The right side of his body, from the lungs down went numb. He leaned to the left and felt the numbness rain down in a blank slick sheet.

His hand shook as it reached for the patch of adhesive. He glanced over at the EKG and noting his increased heart rate, set his mind to quell it. Three seconds later he was able to tape the IV in a stationary position on his back.

Picking up the scalpel was the hardest thing he had ever done. Was it possible to turn back after the years of preparation? Some of the questions to which he sought "The Answer" presented themselves like his first lover—ready yet apprehensive—to his conscious mind. He chose to proceed.

He would begin with ancillary questions.

First, the question of the male sex drive. What was the source of that feeling in his penis when he saw a pretty girl? He felt the definition of Beauty was in there somewhere and what better way to find out if the anesthetic worked? Lowering the blade to the base of his penis he meant to test for sensitivity, but underestimated the pressure and raised a bubble of a sanguine-colored liquid—blood. Riddley paused to re-estimate his position.

He tapped on the plasma bag that would systematically replace his blood loss. He readjusted the bowl of sponges and flipped the switch on the suction machine. The raspy sucking-in-of-air blended with the electric hum of the lights. Riddley made a slow, precise incision opening to the world his reproductive root. As the suction pump neared the rising pool of blood, Holly Martíne, high-school infatuation, entered his mind. He wanted to write this, but realized he had forgotten to bring a pencil near the operating table. He wondered what else he had forgotten. The blood overflowed onto the table. Remembering, he lowered the hose into the area above the seminal vesicle, clearing the view of the vas deferens. He felt good. Glancing at the monitor, his vital signs proved stable. A quarter-smile turned up on his face.

He recalled the mental picture of Holly and gently poked his bulbourethral gland with the tip of a steel probe. Feeling nothing, Riddley traded the probe for the scalpel and severed the skin which covered the testis. Again the probe proved inconclusive. A bead of sweat dripped into his eye reminding him to check the vitals monitor. Another plane crushed the sky above him. The numbers on the screen indicated a minor need for oxygen. He set the probe in its tray and turned for the oxygen mask when he noticed an hour and nine minutes had elapsed from the wall clock.

If he was to get to the big questions, this folly would have to end. The rush of oxygen dizzied him; his left hand lost grip on the hose. It fell a centimeter out of reach, sucking air and wriggling like a crazy deflating balloon. The blood redoubled. Dropping the mask, peeling one glove, let it fall, Riddley nicked the suction hose with his finger nail (good-luck forgot to trim) increasing the arc of the hose's foreswing and Hey Newton! A welcome homecoming to his sweaty palm.

He cleaned the mess from this minor setback and closed his eyes, thinking a minute would help gain composure. Riddley was startled from his trance by an alarming tone, which signaled the need to change the plasma bag. That minute, which the clock showed lasted ten, fostered disturbing thoughts of Hamlet. Riddley sewed the area with a fastidious hand. The practice on feral cats had justified itself. He wanted to apologize to the cats for the one that died, but the progress of science must not be hampered by diplomacy. As he knotted the last stitch, the clock noted the passing of two hours eighteen minutes.

As Riddley dug into the abdomen with the scalpel he had no hope of finding answers. The initial layers of fat yielded little blood. Riddley set his intestines on a tray designed for that purpose. They shuddered, grumbling, in a quick rolling spasm. He clamped the major veins and arteries, clearing a view of the organs around the incision. He stretched the opening to the limit of the skin's elasticity and held it with the retractor. His left arm went into the hole half-way to the elbow searching for the liver. This action tickled Riddley, though he couldn't identify where the feeling came from. He checked the anesthesia delivery system. He smiled. Grasping the liver brought forth a spurt of black bile which made an interesting blot on the white linen that draped the operating table. Riddley thought the spots looked like gloating cockroaches. He had forgotten the question he meant to pose the liver. Although the vitals monitor didn't call for it, Riddley applied oxygen. He was overcome by a rush of hatred… [He paused and lost the thought.] In the liver he found despair.

No truth was found in either kidney, bladder, nor pancreas. He felt nothing. Then a flash of insight, in the guise of a question appeared. The best guide to answers were questions. Did the key to humankind's evolutionary mystery lay dormant in the appendix? A picture of a six-year-old in a birthday hat filled his mind with sirens and flashing lights. His appendix was as "la-hong ga-ha-on" as a river on one of the old Hank Williams records his dad played on Sunday morning.

As he paused to change the blood plasma, the image of the ink-blot roaches crept to the forefront of his thoughts. Riddley despised that the roach would outlive humankind. Yet he admired the way they'd evolved to survive our petty armageddons.

His stomach was a purple-ish brown sack of yellow acids that fizzed in tune with the electric hum of the lights and the purr of the suction pump. He dragged the point of the probe across the surface of the dreary planet. Billions were spent on space travel when The Answer was somewhere beneath this casement of seismic activity. Riddley was hungry. He reached over into the refrigerator. Next to the remaining bags of blood plasma was a bottle of Beer (generic) and a plum. Three hours and twenty-seven minutes had passed. Riddley wanted to pour the beer into his stomach, but recalled that he was saving it for his fiancé. The vitals monitor informed Riddley that the cold bottle in his palm was lowering his body temperature. His grip slackened. The bottle slipped, crashing on the floor, sending a piece of brown glass skidding under the oven where it severed a cockroach. The pathetic front half of the bug dragged into the open and was drowned in a flood of frothy golden death.

Revelation had come. Humankind needed an enemy to brunt its violent nature. Unity rested in struggle against the roach! Salvation could be ours. He didn't expect that word ours, that plural pronoun. Riddley struggled to unify himself. What happened to mine? Mine. Relaying the intestines like a mason, removing the clamps, counting the sponges, like sheep in a dream, fumble-juggling the second-to-last plasma bag onto the hook, thinning the anesthetic as time rushed away, sewing like mom-on-your-costume-an-hour-before-the class-play because you forgot.

A little before midnight, six hours and fifty-four minutes after the endeavor had begun the pain rushed through Riddley Harroway's hinges and sinews resplendent. His self-autopsy raised him from the dead.

The loss of consciousness to sleep was imminent. If only he had a pencil to scratch down The Answer so he wouldn't lose it. Ours. Ours. Hours. He scanned the room in vain, his eyes blurred and he passed out.

The next morning the cheerful song of the lark stirred him from sleep. His body ached. The ache of life. He looked at the blood and bile stained sheets, the dirty scattered tools, the blinking machinery. The electric hum of the lights was still with him. His mind was absent of lucid thought, except for the pain. He could remember little of the previous night. As his head tilted in dejection, he fixed on the bloated corpse of the roach belly up in the puddle of spilt beer.

Roaches, he thought. I have roaches?

As soon as he could walk, Riddley Harroway quit his job at the Medical Center and filled out an application at Terminix. He hoped they would give him his own truck.

# GOING TO THE MAT

Most people think laundry is a chore they'd rather not do, but I like the laundry mat. I also like to ride the city bus, so that tells you something about me. The mat is a gathering place. Being thirty, I had to go to the dictionary to find the "mat" in Laundromat™ originates from a trademark. Like Kleenex™. Or Band-aid™. Or Jacuzzi™. I think it's funny clothes become laundry before and after the event of washing. I like to watch the clothes turn in the big dryer with the glass window. The dryer in your home probably has an opaque steel door, so it's no wonder you despise laundry like math homework. Watching the colors spin as the wet clothes tumble is meditation. A blur of red, a flash of pink, moving as a solid circle to the eye, twisting and rolling over, black panties briefly press against the glass integrating with her slacks and my Hawaiian shirt. Lugging, sorting, loading, and folding gives a man a sense of work. I have sweated enough my jeans and T-shirt will need to be washed. Body Odor is forbidden. You won't find rich people at the laundry mat, which is fine because I don't like to look at them. I'm against work, in the poetic spirit of Li Po, but I accept a certain amount is necessary to get to that moment when I have nothing to do but watch the laundry spin.

I pushed a quarter into the slot and the meter blipped from 00 to 15. Another made 30. I put way too many clothes in the dryer, to draw out my meditation. I could have used three or four dryers, but I believe my state of well-being profits from using one. I stared into the laundry vortex to gather my thoughts.

You might not think of the mat as a gathering place. It isn't like the barbershop or even the bar where rum-tipplers and gin-swillers discuss sports or politics. The laundry mat is also a solitary place where a woman or man is forced to connect with her or his clothes in a new, deeper way. The act of making clean is a personal one. Yet, since I go to the same mat in my neighborhood, I often run into friends. One day I saw Pineapple who was a professional skateboarder in the 70s and who played drums in one of my favorite bands in the 90s. I thought he'd dropped out of the scene, but as I saw him folding his wife's sweatshirt and tiny baby pajamas with the feet in them, I realized he'd moved to a later stage in his life. Domestication happens to the best of us. We talked about the good times and exchanged phone numbers, knowing we'd never call, realizing the next time we'd meet would be here at the laundry mat.

I can feel my socks balmy inside my canvas Converse.

I've seen my friend Janice at the laundry mat three times. It's like our laundry cycles flow together. Janice is an anarchist, so she's good at meetings. Though not the kind of person who does laundry at three o'clock on Thursdays. Janice ran for congress in the last election under the Peace & Freedom banner. She's got a tattoo of the biceps-flexing Westinghouse Woman on her own flexed biceps. You might think she stuffs the clean clothes into the rucksack she toted them over in all helter-skelter, since her clothes are mostly old band T-shirts and cut off jeans with holy knees, but she takes care folding each item. She has a good relationship with her laundry.

The laundry mat is both a chaotic, exciting place and a peaceful, contemplative place. The washers roar like intermittent waterfalls, hum and rumble in symphony. The dryer emits a pleasant odor and heat. Small children play on the folding table or run under mama's skirt hem. They climb on the machines looking for coins shucked loose of pockets. I tried to sit on one of the machines and read a book, only to be distracted by a beautiful woman folding her G-string and a rockabilly hipster I didn't know from the club scene folding his boxer shorts. The laundry mat is an intimate exhibition. Sometimes you see stains on bed sheets or crusty stiff hand towels. The imagination frolics.

An old rag Dallas poet Clebo Rainey used to sandbag a bloody nose when he spent the night at my place during his last tour wound up with my dirty clothes. Even though it was a kind of artifact of the art world, I decided to throw it away.

There's bad music piped in. Mellow hits of Manilow. And someone has gone crazy with prohibitions in my laundry mat. One sign reads No Smoking. No Dyeing. Do not sit on machines. Another says No Loitering. Every once in awhile, like today, you see a skinny bum in his dirty skivvies. His one shirt, pants, and socks swirling around in the hot water. He borrowed a cup of soap, accepting it with a two-tooth grin. A bottle in a crisp brown sack waited under the bench. He would probably appreciate a shave. And a bath. He waited for another pilgrim to come out of the coin-op toilet, lunged for the door before it shut. He emerged fifteen minutes later, face scrubbed pink, hair combed with water.

One time I came to the mat with my girl. This insane deaf woman howled like a guttural beast. ACK. ACK. ACK. First I thought she was trying to warn me against losing a fiver in the change machine. I saw she was wearing a sweatshirt, but… ah… there it is… no pants. Her legs were like naked diabetics hoisting a midget to reach the dryer. Apparently she didn't want me to see her in this state of half-undress. It's okay I wanted to say. I was born naked. My girl panicked and loaded our laundry into the triple-loader buck-fifty machine, so we wouldn't have to go on the deaf woman's side where the cheaper machines sat unused.

Outside, in front of the bank, a man preached to the traffic, holding a bible in one hand. His thick lips mouthed scripture, possessed. He was wearing a long-sleeve white dress shirt and red tie. The whites of his eyes looked yellow. The muscles and veins in his throat were like corrugated aluminum as he gestured to heaven summoning brimstone for the heathens. Safe inside the mat, I felt like I was watching a silent movie. Yet, the film credits superimposed on the window—Coin-Op Laundry—appeared to me in reverse, so maybe I was in the film and he was watching me. Hmmm. No. The real drama was unfolding outside. I noticed a bulge at his hip, could it be a gun? Sweat glistened on the preacher's brow as his lips form the word G-E-E-S-U-S.

Janice was telling me about one of the times Emma Goldman was run out of San Diego on a rail. Her lover Ben Reitman, "The Hobo Doctor," suffered a tar and sage-brush beating by twelve men, a vigilante mob, at the behest of our civic leaders. The bosses didn't want them to organize workers. One supposes these are the businessmen the streets are named after Spreckels, Kettner... History fails to name them likely because they owned the newspaper. One, described as a "doctor" himself, seared the initials IWW on Reitman's asscheek with a cigar... The laundry spun. A girl found a dime in a washer, dropped it—clink—and set it rolling across the linoleum. Her little brother chased it—DONG—bumping his noggin on one of the machines, but stopping the coin with a quick shoe slap before it disappeared into the place where errant socks go. His sister pounced on him with a tiny fist gripping a shock of black hair. Gimmie it, the girl said. The mother delivered a searing scold with her eyes without ceasing to fold a red towel. The struggle continued, but more quietly. The bum lifted his shirt, one black sock, a pair of baggy trousers, and another sock from the washer. The mother stacked the red towel on a black one. The preacher drew the gun.

A balding man (clutching a brown briefcase to his chest) stepped out of the bank, looking surprised as the street preacher stepped up, bible in his left hand, pistol in his right. Janice pointed, one hand cupped over her mouth in shock aghast. The street preaching cheetah slapped the bald man with his bible knocking the briefcase to the asphalt. The bald man's head jerked left to a stop. The children seemed to have worked it out; they giggled, unaware. The preacher tucked the bible inside the briefcase. Pistol held godward. Janice looked at me. I shrugged. I wished the deaf woman had been here to read their lips. The man from the bank reached out for the case. His fingertips dragging the length of the preacher's tie. The preacher pushed him, leveled the pistol, and our silent movie broke the sound barrier—CRACK—with the quick report of the gun. We watched the man's back blown out onto the street. The preacher turned and ran. The man from the bank seemed to pursue his assailant. Something valuable must have been in that case. Blood gushed out both sides of the hole in his body. He took four strides before falling on the fifth. The preacher leaped into the passenger side of a Geo Metro. I thought it was green but Janice called it blue. The driver sped away. The bum slipped out the back. The digital meter on my dryer clicked from 01 to 00. It wound to a stop. The clothes dropped—in a heap with a thump—like a body onto the street.

## PAIN IN THE NECK

In 1978, I was in seventh grade. I'd been playing third base for my Little League team. A line drive snags in the web of my heavy leather mitt, that long throw across the diamond sails over the first baseman's head toward the other team's dugout. A runner comes around to score. It's my fault. I've disappointed everyone. I've lost the game. My dad hangs on the backstop with nervous anticipation weighing on his face. Mom's at home washing the dishes or at a movie with my sister.

A few days after one of the games, I complained to my mom about an acute pain in my neck. It's nothing honey, she said. You strained it playing ball. I didn't remember any incidents, any injuries that could have caused this particular pain though my skinned knee stung from a rugged slide into second. Any pain from the whomping our team suffered at the bats of our rivals had passed by the time we raced to the field snack bar waving a ticket. Each day the neck pain got worse until I couldn't get out of bed. Mom! I yelled. This was before She's fallen and can't get up played over and over on a TV commercial. All the kids had long hair because we were surfers and the older kids on the block were stoners. This was before I discovered punk rock. The kids across the street were into Kiss but my favorite band was Cheap Trick singing, Mommy's all right, Daddy's all right, they just seem a little weird.

The doctor said, You probably strained a muscle playing baseball. I protested to no avail that there was no injury. Let's try physical therapy, he said. Each day the pain got worse. It may get worse before it gets better. I couldn't turn my head from side to side, and I couldn't lift from laying down. The therapist was nice enough. She had this industrial vibrating massager and gelatin. It could have been ultrasound; did they have ultrasound? She worked that thing into my back and shoulders. I wish I had that hummer now to try on my girlfriend. That hurts, I told her. She probably thought I was another wimpy kid who would man up when he got real problems. SNAP! The therapist heard it; my mom heard it; and I felt it. The crisp snap of my neck breaking. Of course, I screamed. Hysterically. I screamed like they'd murdered the child inside of me. Rushed to the adjacent hospital and strapped into traction, kinda like one of those machines at the gym with a harness attached to iron weights cradling my head to keep my neck immobile.

Immobility was where it was at.

All they could tell me was my neck was broken. The doctors discarded the Little League injury hypothesis. Why this healthy twelve-year-old boy was lying immobile in a hospital was a total mystery. Doctors and nurses stood over me with puzzled expressions. They put me in the children's ward because misery loves company. I shared the room with tonsillectomies and mummy-bandaged burn victims. One kid visiting his sister in the next ward felt so sorry for me he gave me a first edition Iron Man. I got to know the bedpan and fear the sponge bath. The doctors ran tests and I was known for the months of June, July, and, August as The Human Pin Cushion of Room 842B. Every few hours a nurse or technician came at me with a needle. The spearpoint skin pop, the plunger forces or draws some burning liquid into or from my bloodstream. If they could find a vein, they took blood three times a day, shot me full of isotopes, and plugged IVs into me like TVs into the socket. One of the IVs left this now-faint quarter-inch scar on my left hand. I spent most of my time watching the TV through these prism glasses they gave me (since I had to lie flat staring at the ceiling in traction). The prisms turned the lights into rainbows.

The doctors figured out I had a blood disease called Eosynophyllic Granuloma. Everyone seemed impressed I could say Eosynophyllic Granuloma. A biopsy left my third cervical vertebra destroyed, so they installed what is known as a halo cast: a steel halo that orbits your skull physically screwed and bolted into the bone with four bolts—two at the temples and two in the back. They had to shave my head, so technically I had the first punk hairstyle at school.

Steel rods came down from the halo secured to a plaster cast that covered my entire slight torso. The abrasions left scars where the cast rubbed my hip bones. The worst part was that the bolts had to be tightened once a week with a long torque wrench. Turning the bolt felt like what I imagine diving too deep in the ocean feels like. My head being crushed like an aluminum can.

The halo offered mobility. I could walk around like Frankenstein with the added bonus of small children bursting into tears at the sight of me. Radiation destroyed the remnants of the tumor (time will tell what else). The first day of seventh grade was a trip. My mom worked as a keypunch operator in a sweatshop run by Ross Perot, a funny little man who ran for President with sophisticated charts to illustrate his plans. My dad worked like so many dads in those days making war machines for the Cold War. So I rode the handicap bus to school. The short bus of contemporary lore. I shared the ride with Special Ed students drooling and screaming in wheelchairs, surviving the year with successively smaller braces until in the end, I had to wear a foam rubber whiplash collar. I was glad to be rid of the braces because there were sweaty, dank, and musty places on my pubescent body that hadn't been washed in a long time.

Many years later (after causing my mother insurmountable worry about my neck with slam dancing and skateboarding and jumping off buildings into pools) I got a teaching credential from the university and worked as a substitute teacher. One of my long term assignments was to teach Special Ed. These were the kids I shared the bus with in seventh grade. They ranged from droolers and screamers who had to be fed through a tube to the mentally deranged. There was a kid named Angel who would follow me around campus. He would wait for me by the parking lot in the morning and stand outside the teacher's lounge at lunch. The other teachers thought it was cute. Mr. J, your secret admirer is outside. Mr. J, your follower is here. Angel looked like a normal kid, except his mother cut his thick black hair with a cereal bowl template so he looked a bit like Antonin Artaud in Jeanne d'Arc. Angel could do some school work and carry a conversation. I liked him better than some of the teachers. Yet, there was something strange. His disability, I suspected, was a sociopathic disorder. He would creep right into your space like a pesky vine to creepy-crawl your nerves. He scrutinized missing buttons on my shirts, distinguished freckles from moles from warts. He announced when wrinkles appeared and told me about my first gray hair. He wanted me for a friend, I guess, invited me to a jazz concert and wanted me to take him somewhere, anywhere, away from his home on the weekend, which teachers do not do and I never did. His family were Jehovah's Witnesses. He was always talking about Jesus or

God, but mostly about the Devil. Once he said, If I saw the Devil, I would kill him.

Would he go to heaven? I replied.

No, he would go to Hell. Angel's voice was a creepy whisper, like everything he said was a secret between me and him.

Why don't you just tell the Devil to go home? I said. He didn't laugh, I don't remember him laughing; he simply absorbed my words like gospel.

The conversation repeated slightly varied each day. Hey, I said. If you killed the Devil, that would be murder and you would go to hell too.

He assembled the words in that statement like a puzzle. He found the edge pieces and considered them trying to construct meaning.

A few days later, he whispered, I think you're the Devil with a dead serious carved-from-stone face. He pointed at the twin scars on my forehead above my temples saying, That's where you cut off your horns.

I smiled and replied, That's where they cut off my halo.

## GREAT GIVING OF THANKS

I'm fascinated with the point things start to go wrong. Sociologists analyze events, like school shootings, to find the moment where the tragedy might have been averted by the nudge of one detail. If A hadn't abused B who bullied C, then D, E, F, G, H & I might be alive. But I am not a sociologist. Let it be a given that my friends and I are inveterate drunkards and the consumption of alcohol played its usual role. But there has to be more to this story than alcohol in, violence out.

In the comic books, Bruce Banner is able to morph into The Incredible Hulk because of exposure to gamma radiation. But why does he gets so angry? Wherefore art thou, rage? Alaska seems to have an interest to actively keep my flaming ire in check. I'm no longer allowed, for example, to yell at cars that encroach the crosswalk and almost kill us. I've never planned to scream at a car. It's not conscious. The lion roars. I can claim I scream at cars to wake the driver from the sleep of habit, but Alaska sees this as a post hoc rationalization. She's playing a longer game. If something violent dwells therein, ready to kill, maybe I should hold on to it.

I know, I know. This was supposed to be a festival of thanks. We gathered friends to count the blessings of another bountiful harvest, another year survived. But Thanksgiving has always been genesis and genocide. A cornucopia of feast and famine, birth and murder. A wedding and a wake. Thanksgiving is a dark harvest where bad corn comes in with the good. We celebrate life but must reckon with all that drags it down—the debilitating nature of work, the deleterious effect of daily lives enslaved by banality, and any number of etching scintilla that manifest fear. We live a Gulf of Tonkin away from war, always, inundated by rent rising like a river, on a planet slowly warming toward catastrophe. Our fascination with the zombie apocalypse means something. Get ready. Shoot for the head. Or join the brain eaters. The brain-eaters are coming in the form of the homeless, hurricanes, the aging elderly. The corner street preacher decries the end of days. Poverty, bird flu, asteroid strike, locusts, supervolcanoes… the existential threats are vast.

Last year on Thanksgiving we drove to Alaska's mom's house then my mom's then home. The year before the "loop-lap" took us north 72.2 miles for brunch with the moms, 65.4 miles west across the busiest freeway in the world for dinner at my dad's, followed by the stop-and-go slog 78.5 miles home.

Every year on this day 46 million turkeys are slaughtered.

Hey Dad, do you want to come to our apartment this year for Vegan Thanksgiving?

I'm sorry son, but we don't want to drive in the holiday traffic.

Hi Mom. Do you want to come for Thanksgiving? Alaska and Ariadne Arkadyevna planned a terrific meal with seitan pot pie and sweet potato pie and pumpkin pie.

Is there going to be turkey?

No.

Well, I'm going to my successful son's house for turkey.

Just like that, we felt free to assert our adulthood by staying home. Well, I felt free. Alaska compounded the guilt she felt about leaving her mother alone on the holiday with a lie meant to spare feelings.

Mama, you should go to Thanksgiving with someone in the church. We can't drive up this year because Jimmy has to work early.

Richard Mitchell, aka Tricky Dick Mitchell, sometimes called Richie, Mitch, Mitchell, Rich Mitch, Dick and rarely, but sometimes "a royal dick," was the only full-fledged carnivore we invited, but I don't think this had anything to do with what happened. If he was pissed about not getting turkey, like my mom, he never mentioned it. Dick, for someone who has no use for most human beings, is surprisingly good at parties, at small talk, at holding forth, at least before his motor faculty for speech fails. His girlfriend, Helga Kropotkin, cooked vegan at home, so he was used to finding his own meat.

Alaska and Ariadne made four pot pies, a green bean casserole pie, a sweet potato pie, stuffing from a box, mashed potatoes, and garlic gravy. I like those gelatinous cranberries that retain the shape of the can my mom used to slide onto a plate, but Ariadne likes to make cranberry sauce from scratch with lots of sugar. Cecil Hayduke brought a curried lentil and yam pie, announcing, Cecil can cook, in an uncharacteristic expression of pride after a highball of Scotch whisky and the first glass of sangria, which Helga brewed over a cauldron with an unspeakable recipe passed down the female line of her generations. Bridgette and Otto brought a side of wild rice, even though they'd spent the better part of the day at Bridgette's mother's house stuffing themselves with vegetarian side dishes while the rest of their family ate turkey.

This party is turning out to be a full-time job, Bridgette said about four hours in. I saw the next day my computer played songs for eight hours, repeating one tune Cecil wanted to hear again. The first 100 played randomly before I got drunk and relived my college radio days. Wudang Shan, from next-door, stepped in for sangria with Margot, who lived in a small house behind our place. I played The Jam, The Clash, The Damned. Our upstairs neighbor,

Memo Santiago, wasn't into the punk rock but started to really shake it down when The Hot 8 Brass Band tuba'd-forth *Sexual Sexual Sexual Healing*. Cecil and I sang along with Daniel Johnston *Got me a coffin, shiny and black, going to a funeral and I'm never coming back.* Alaska and I stomped up a sweat to a set of The Specials, The Selector, and The Dancehall Crashers. And I played Jawbreaker *If I had a million bucks…* because Helga had traveled with them working the merch table.

I think that cliché about avoiding politics and religion at Thanksgiving mostly applies to family. Like when we drive up to see my dad Alaska says, We need to program ourselves to avoid taboo subjects. We try but it never works. Veritably, his wife opens the door, and, veritably, I swagger through armed with a quiver of reasons. When she says, I don't believe in global warming, or I don't believe in evolution, I can't seem to restrain a response.

That's crazy. You don't have to believe in evolution. Scientists don't believe in it. They test it. And so far after thousands and thousands of tests conducted by thousands of scientists, evolution has never been proven wrong. The genius of science is that, like Einstein v. Newton, when someone finds a fact that proves a theory wrong, we abandoned it. Looking up from my lecture, I might have seen the tear coming down her cheek from the moment "I called her crazy."

But the outrageous confessions our friends made across Thanksgiving didn't have the same effect on us. We argued, and minds failed to change, which on reflection is depressing, but with music, wine, and new topics exploding all around we didn't have time for reflection.

I'm not a feminist, Jennifer said.

I'm probably still a Catholic, Hazel said.

Nimby liberal lameness is the endemic quality of all Democrats, Dick shouted.

Clinton is a Republican cunt who voted for every war that came across her path, believes in the death penalty, and wants to help her rich friends get richer, Cecil added. The lameness is endemic to democracy. Voting is stupid, it makes you lazy.

Otto, who has a strange mind, capped by a Tyrollean hat, went to the backyard, scraped lichen off the lemon tree to illustrate a point he was trying to make about symbiotic relationships. Helga and Bridgette bonded over a fascination with mycelium. And since I'd just read Carl Zimmer's book, I regaled my friends with stories of parasites worming into our brains to control everything. They could drive ants like golf carts, change the gender of crabs, and push a rat into a feline maw by paralyzing its sense of fear.

This cheesecake is delicious.

It's tofu.

Really?

Ya.

Typical American cultural appropriation, Wudang declared. But delicious.

Palm oil is killing apes.

Thanksgiving is bullshit.

Global warming has opened the Northwest Passage.

Your crucifix was made in a Chinese sweatshop.

Thanks for a continent to despoil and poison.

Dick Cheney is the worst human on earth.

His bloodthirst in unquenchable... biggest crime since Vietnam what they did in Iraq.

There are always worse humans waiting in the wings.

I'm going to study in the bedroom, Ariadne said retreating from the "adult" world, leaving us to our talk and drink. Alaska, of course, went to look in on her.

She's napping.

No napping! Memo shouted. It's Thanksgiving.

Whaddya mean? Napping is a huge part of Thanksgiving.

I'm in a food coma.

That's what cocaine is for.

Shut up. Memo thundered up the echoing stairwell to his apartment and whatever the next person said was drowned by a blast from a trumpet.

In order to prevent our friends from coagulating into cliques, Alaska ushered them onto two couches and two folding chairs in our living room. The red leather couch was the first piece of furniture that wasn't handed down or found in an alley. The other, upholstered gold, which had been found in an alley, was still in pristine condition. The forced proximity in our one-bedroom apartment probably had a lot to do with what happened. The significance of the first splash of spilled wine and first broken glass was amplified by close quarters. But like the old Casbah where 150 rockers crammed in a space for half that, close-quarters build exultation.

Two-day party!

Jazz called two-day party, nobody leaves.

Hey Jazz, where are you going man?

The clock read two am, so I thought it prudent to go out the front door in search of my daughter, who hadn't returned after walking her boyfriend to his car. I wanted to take Armand's keys and tell him to crash on the couch, but he must have parked on a side street, or perhaps they'd driven off. I stumbled into The Crack Den, which was my name for the house on the corner where a bunch of "quiet punks" lived. They tried to name their flop Tree House, which will have to stand, Crack Den having fallen into disfavor after the death by misadventure of one of the roommates.

Oxy and whisky don't mix.

James, who played drums in Trashcan Fires, was sitting in the bower with three sleepy revelers staring into a fire pit's diminishing embers—the roommate who rented the hammock in the eponymous tree looked ominous, face cut by shadow; Lizi-Lu Corbin squeezed the last notes out of an accordion and Franklin Steinbeck was explaining his plan to join the Free Masons.

Sorry I couldn't stop Helen coming over.

She was so wasted.

Yeah, we manufactured bad drunks over there tonight.

No problem man. We made a few of our own. Genevieve came out of the bedroom and made a rule against shrill screaming.

Some night.

Yeah.

Yeah.

Where's Cecil?

Asleep in his car. I pointed.

No shit. Ha.

Helen Highwater had come over from her shift at Sparky's. When I took the bottle out of her hand because Dick, flailing and grabbing for everything almost knocked it over, she thought I was trying to cut her off.

I got it back. LOL, she said pulling it close against her breast.

Just trying to save the sofa, Doll.

You have to write that book, Doll.

Tell me how it ends, Doll. Have you decided to quit drinking? Because all the played out chronicles of "booze, drugs, and crazy sex" end in death or rehab, or rehab rehab rehab death.

Who cares? she shouted pouring maintenance sippers into a glass from the bottle.

Alaska how much older are you than Jimmy Jazz?

A year.

Eleven months.

I'm three years older than Otto, Bridgette said.

I've got seven on Wudang Shan, Margot said.

Helga's ten years older than Dick, Cecil said.

Dick reaches for someone's drink; Helga pays him no mind.

Hazel, who didn't have a boyfriend, set her eye on Memo's ex-Marine friend sipping a beer in the corner.

Okay, well listen Dolls. I'm 38 and this boy I invited over is twenty-one, so be careful with him.

He's a baby.

Welcome to The Cougar Den, Cecil said.

Alaska's phone rang. It was Helen. I'm walking from Sparky's and there are some scary looking guys on the corner of 29th.

We'll come out.

I set my sangria on the porch step. Alaska stayed on the phone until we spotted her silhouette.

Is she weaving?

Could be us.

Hi, Dolls.

My legs felt heavy climbing the steps. Where's my sangria? *The Turkish Song of the Damned* played inside.

Sounds like a good party.

So far.

Alaska opened a white wine because Helen had sworn off red along with the hard stuff after her first DUI. I can't drink Crown at the end of the night any more Dolls. Helen is always calling people Doll or Champ. She's one of those day-drinking believers, like a Xtian doting on heaven, switching from brown liquor to clear or red wine to Bud Lite.

Does this young boy know what he's getting into?

He's seen more crazy shit in the past two weeks... but he keeps coming for more. He's not one of the downtown boys if you know what I mean. I feel like I've been riding a horse for the past two days. He's an outdoor type, we're going camping. Can you imagine me camping? Where will I get a slice a pizza? He said to leave the $1000 handbag and heels at home. LOL. Alaska can I borrow some sneakers? He promised a cooler full of Bud Lite so I'm game. No more slapping though.

He's trying to control you already. A loser's game.

Didn't you say it isn't even sex without slapping?

Young guys don't like getting slapped, at least across the face.

Margot let out a cougar growl; Bridgette, Hazel, and Jennifer joined in. Alaska heard the growls from the kitchen; Helga sat on the couch and took a sip from her wine.

When he comes in pause the music and everybody look at him.

No-o-o-o! Helen slurred.

Don't be an ass Jimmy. Give the kid a break.

Earlier in the day, I was telling Dick and Helga my sense of humor had been surprising me. The public persona putting on a show or the writer creating drama. Cecil might call this an aspect of my usual boring introspection. When I told him I was writing this story he said that after correcting the spelling I should use the Microsoft Self-Pity Checker. I've known Helen 10 years, Helga 18, Alaska 24, and Ariadne her entire life. They haven't dumped me yet, so... To paraphrase the poet Michael Klam, absent from this party, which me was it who smiled holding the door while the paramedics wheeled my boss out on a gurney? Schadenfreude me? Which me was it who said, yesterday, to that same boss, Have fun tomorrow at IHOP? As far as I'm concerned she reaps what she sows and her misery is my pleasure. Rat-dissector me. Alaska thinks I inherited a cruel humor from my mother who called to say how good the turkey was at her successful son's house. She calls her boss at Michael's craft store her successful son because he's a boss and owns a limo business on the side. A dubious prospect, inheriting mother's cowlicked locks and stepping-razor humor while our attitudes about bosses and owners diverge so completely. I must have gotten the recessive gene for anti-authoritarianism.

Assholes say they were making a joke when they hurt someone. Alcoholics blame booze. For the most part, I consider myself a sensitive being who cares about friends and family. Thus anxiety.

About six hours before our vegan feast, pies out of the oven, Alaska, Ariadne, and I hiked Cowles Mountain with Dick and Helga. Helga thought it might be crowded, but I said, On Thanksgiving? No, everyone will be prepping dinner or eating. We ended up in a queue to the summit. A dozen joggers passed us weaving in and around the line of walkers. We were stuck behind an old lady with a huge ass wearing rhinestone glasses walking with Britany in hot pants on her cell phone, on the next switchback a black girl walked a dog, an Asian tourist paused to take a photo slowing the procession, a large Mexican family two switchbacks above shuffled dust... couples with dogs, couples without dogs. Gay men. Three moms with babies. Some fit, some fat. Most sweating. I ran into Mean Steve, a coworker, coming down the trail. I hate that jerk. On a clear day, you can see The Pacific, the downtown, the Coronado Bridge, Mummy Island. But today the haze obscured everything.

Look at that smog on the horizon. Glad we're not breathing it, I said trying to make a joke.

Are there too many people in the world?

Too many on this hill.

We brought five.

Party of five, something on the precipice?

Helga and I used to live on the same street. She teaches at the Community College where Ariadne is enrolled in her English 205 class. I'm not sure how many kids hike with their professors or share holiday meals. Alaska and Dick stopped to let two college girls pass. I don't want to live in the dorms next year, one said. There are too many freshmen all excited about helping out in the community. Ha, Dick laughed whispering, Her T-shirt said Students for Social Justice.

On Black Friday, I asked my daughter for her thoughts about the party. You guys are weird, she said. In a good way. And who knows how other people act when we're not looking. Cecil said on the phone, Those kids aren't shocked by our behavior; they have way crazier parties. I was walking to the curb with a piece of pie for Cecil this morning, but the rev and rumble of a trash truck distracted me. By the time I pushed our can into the alley and came out with the pie, he was gone.

Helga called around ten to say Dick got into the house. Great party, she said laughing. Helga laughs often, deeply, and well, but in this case, I wasn't sure if it was with or at me. Dick seems like he's exercising selective memory about last night. I think he remembers more than he's saying.

No dude. The trash will not resume until Monday.

You have never had a properly cooked Brussels sprout.

Our parents and grandparents didn't cook.

Fucking TV dinners.

Belgium doesn't even claim Brussels sprouts. They blame the French.

Le petite choux, a relative of the cabbage.

I can't get passed a childhood aversion to one vegetable because I like its cousin.

No man we can't play Fugazi; we need to play something softer so Dick will mellow the fuck out. Cecil retreated, stoned, into the headphones of his MP3 player and pulled on Alaska's sunglasses trying to vanish while remaining at the party.

This is the first year we aren't going to our parents' house for Thanksgiving.

My dad's underground and my mom's in a nursing home.

My internship at the hospital makes me feel like I'm growing up.

It'll feel more like it when you get paid.

I won't get paid until my student loans are settled.

Sorry man, you'll never feel like an adult.

In the Navy, they tell you when to eat and sleep like a child.

I'm afraid of my genes. Will I hole up with a cache of weapons like Dad in Idaho or drink myself insane like Mom in Baltimore?

Did you read that book about Ted Kaczynski?

They did experiments on Dad at Yale too. Fucked him up.

You can get matching shacks in the woods. Oi Cecil, when you brought Krakauer's Into the Wild on our trip to June Lake, I thought it might be a suicide note. I was so glad to see you come limping into camp. Cecil had planned to backpack on the ridge leaving Alaska, Helga, and I at the campground with bathrooms and fire rings. He made fun of us for packing three kinds of alternative milk. Up mountain, he pulled a groin, hitched a ride back in a truck.

You and Dick always played rough. Remember the 4th of July when he wanted to show you his wrestling skills.

You yelled, Stop! as he slammed me on the grass. Louis Jordan's *Saturday Night Fish* Fry came on and Alaska and I cut the rug with our unique hybrid of Western Swing and London Pogo.

I think Dick was self-medicating after the hike. He drank a six-pack talking to his sister on the phone.

Everyone I checked in with speculated about Dick's sudden and debilitating drunk. Did he take pills? Was he on X? Check your medicine cabinet. Did Helen give him a Valium? Helen sold Cecil two Valiums. I bet Helen gave him a Valium.

He was being a royal dick; I'm surprised he didn't get punched sooner.

Dick danced to the songs spitting out of my computer. He turned his back to the interlocutors, swaying, wavering. Lanky arms, like albatross wings, gliding the length of the gold sofa. Middle and index fingers poised in a curious gesture. Pointing this way, then that.

My stepmother claims never to have been drunk nor to have seen anyone drunk.

She should have been here.

Do you think having a real adult present would have changed the outcome?

Na, man. Everybody drank too much sangria. And the bottles of wine opened. Armand Tuscadero's family gave you that pot of Swedish Glögg for Xmas last year. You can't give the gift of alcohol and expect people not to drink it.

It's like that time we got thrown out of the Drunk Poets Society for being drunk. Cheers to us all. Your stepmom woulda gotten plowed.

We didn't drink at my dad's Thanksgiving, though he had two Amstel Lites waiting in the fridge. He said he got them for me, but I couldn't drink them because, aside from being a beer snob, he didn't get anything for Alaska. Was she supposed to sip cranapple juice and watch me knock them back?

You could have each had one.

Ha. What's the point of one beer?

Some people like the taste.

Of Amstel?

Your dad drinks one glass of wine in the evening now, my grandmother said. In front of the TV.

I don't watch TV grandma.

Well, why not, darlin?

Because it makes you stupider. Oops, did I say that to my 86-year old grandma who likes to watch World Series of Poker? I meant it makes me stupider. I prefer books.

God bless you, darlin'.

So you think Jesus was black? my step-mother asked.

No, I think Jesus is a composite fictional character, a repository for proverbial sayings, not a historical person.

I brought the Amstels home thinking Helen might drink them, but Cecil got there first.

So I was drunk sitting at the controls of my computer playing Cannibal and the Headhunters, Ritchie Valens, Jimmy Liggins, Eddie Cochrane, Jerry Lee Lewis, Little Richard, Los Teen Tops, and Sister Rosetta Tharpe, just rocking out. Leaping up to do the mashed potato. Twisting, Shouting. Our friend Sonny came over and ate a plate of food and got high with Cecil. After that Cecil was so wasted he sat on the couch wearing the sunglasses. Everyone was drunk. Margot and Wudang Shan, and Memo from upstairs looked like they were feeling alright. Bridgette and Otto said goodbye (they probably weren't drunk and neither was Memo's girlfriend, Jennifer, the art student). Alaska lost track after three sangrias.

Ariadne came out of the bedroom. Helen was swimming in alcohol; Dick was pestering her, even though an eerie aphasia seized his vocal cords and he could only communicate by reaching his long arms out for things.

Back off man! Helen said. If you were single I'd throw you

down on the sofa right now. You've got a girlfriend man, so back off.

I wasn't groping her, Dick told Helga the next day. Helen was wearing my ski vest and I wanted my wallet out of the breast pocket. So I had pulled Dick away from Helen and he was pulling on my satin smoking jacket. I forgot to say I had slicked my hair back and was wearing a satin smoking jacket for the dinner party. Several people mentioned this image the next day. The satin smoking jacket and the mood light. The room was lit with candles and a red light bulb, and the fluorescent desk lamp my grandma gave me, the one she says has had the same bulb since 1968. I've had it for eight years and haven't changed it. So Dick was tugging at the smoking jacket and I was trying to get him seated. Like toast, I'd push him down and he'd pop up. People were changing positions in the room as if in the strobe light. With Velvet Underground traveling music, Andy Warhol could have made a fascinating film about transitions. A film in search of lost time.

Alcohol, as Einstein said, warps time and space.

Not Ari! Helen screamed. Hands off. He was tugging Ariadne's arm. As he was lumbering about the room, Alaska and I cleared the empty glasses and moved them to the kitchen. We insist on the right glass for the right occasion. So there were wine glasses, martini glasses, pint glasses, and tiny snifters half full of Glögg strewn among the empty bottles.

Helga was on the couch plotting Buy Nothing Day stop shopping interventions with Cecil. The best laid plans of the stoned and hammered. Neither got up early enough to stop traffic at the mall or march through a big box store dressed as a zombie. Right before Dick lost the ability to speak, he told us about the class project where he rented a priest outfit, inspired by Rev. Billy, and chanted hellfire and rainforest depletion at the Starbucks kitty-corner from his favorite mom and pop café.

Shit, I gotta pick up my watch at the repair shop tomorrow, Dick remembered.

Having something repaired in the age of Chuck-it-n-buy-a-new-one earns a pass, Cecil granted. No worries.

The Pope of Stop Shopping hands out indulgences.

When Helen's 21-year old boy knocked at the door the first thing he saw was Dick crawling on the rug with the long arm and two pointed fingers extending. The music was playing full volume. Jazz, Jazz, Cecil cried. Get him off me. I tried to stop him from pulling on Cecil's leg which he'd broke last year slipping on ice plant to take out the garbage. Dick had known this, but we were starting to wonder who was driving the robot drunken maniac. I guided him back on the couch. Helen put a drink in the kid's hand. Soon enough Dick was bumping into people, wine spilling. I wiped one spill only to see another across the room. Not the gold sofa! I remember looking at Helga and wondering why she didn't control him. She was his cougar after all. Then again why should she be responsible? They weren't married. There had been no vows, no promises. Most married people forgot that shit as they said it anyway. They had lived next door to each other for years sharing stairs and a foyer, but with his and hers deadbolts. They shared cooking and I imagined slept together. But like Ariadne said, Who knows what people do?

About this time Alaska and I were scrambling to clear breakables from the kitchen table. Dick grabbed a wine glass, maybe looking for a bottle to fill it; maybe unconscious it was a glass. It either fell to the floor or crashed against the table. I got the broom and dustpan—drunk myself—bailing the boat. I'm taking The Kid over to the Crack Den, Helen said. Cecil was on the couch listening to Fugazi's *In on the Kill Taker* in his headphones. I was playing *Wee Small Hours of the Morning* and Chet Baker Sings and blowing out candles because what about fire and sweeping glass and playing *Lady Sings the Blues*. Trying to control with the music. Whatever Plato said about the danger of music controlling people was dumb. Drunks cannot be controlled; they march and flail to a private rhythm pitches above sobriety.

Ariadne's boyfriend Armand came in, evidently why Ariadne woke to re-join the party.

Don't get too close to these people; they're dangerous.

Cecil on the couch with his sunglasses.

Helen staggering out the door.

Dick groping for his lost ability to speak.

Can I have a beer? Since it was a holiday, I thought one beer (the last) wouldn't hurt him, which highlights my lack of maturity or level of inebriation. I found out minutes later he'd been drinking 40s in the park with friends and left his parents' house after they accused him of being on drugs.

I might get kicked out, he said. Play a Bad Brains song for me. My parents want me to take a drug test. Play Bad Brains.

Hello. I believe our kids are dating. Were you aware that they've been alone together while we were at work? Don't worry, we put a stop to that.

They're adults; Ariadne's on the pill.

Armand's parents had returned from South Africa where Mr. Tuscadero flew bibles to tribes in the bush. Alaska ran into him at Mervyn's. Armand doesn't say much, at least not to us. He had a job at a bookstore, read Kerouac, quit the bookstore, and gutted fish in Alaska over the summer. I should have known he was high as he was not only talking with adults but talking shit. The newfound courage running through his veins like bulls through Pamplona was alcohol: $C_nH_{2n+1}OH$. I tried to snatch the beer when Alaska told me he was already loose, but he clutched it like a teddy bear.

Play Bad Brains.

No. I'm trying to keep Rich Mitch here mellow. Mitchell. Too late. Dick grabbed him.

Cool it Huggles. Helga and Cecil remained on the couch, so I pried Dick loose and planted him between them. He got free flailing and clutching, but this time Memo grabbed him.

You look like you need a bearhug there buddy.

Huggles... ha ha let's call him Huggles.

Twenty-four inches, Dick said desperately trying to break his inability to speak.

This son of a bitch is lit up.

Memo sat him down; he nodded off.

Play Bad Brains for me.

Okay, I said putting on *Re-ignition*, which proved an evil portent as Dick rose flailing and pawing.

Helga, did you go to that Bad Brains show in TJ?

It was the best show anyone played there, she said, which was huge considering she'd seen Nirvana and The Ramones. The Bad Brains could create an incredible mix of punk violence cut with interludes of Jain-like tenderness.

I'm not listening to you man, you're wearing sunglasses and it's night.

Jazz Jazz, greatest hardcore band: Bad Brains or Minor Threat?

Black Flag.

No greatest from DC.

Cecil lost interest when Sonny rolled a joint on a book.

Hey, that's a library book.

Dick was massaging Armand's thigh on the gold sofa as Helga and Cecil looked on from the red couch. He was sitting on the back of the sofa extending his long arms out pointing with two fingers and hugging and grabbing everyone.

Hey man I hardly know you, Armand said pushing Dick off. The human functions in the frontal lobe of his cerebral cortex had shut down carrying him back to an atavistically devolved state. Alcohol works against coordination, judgment, speech, and most humans will puke before it shuts off the puking mechanism and the switches for lung and heart function cease. After the kidneys and liver are destroyed the brain hasn't got a chance.

Zombie Dick became obsessed with hugging Armand. Knock it off Huggles. I swear if you kiss me, I'll fucking kill you. Stop. I got up from the DJ chair to pry him loose.

Not the satin smoking jacket. The Zombie fixed his blank gaze on me. I slipped out of the jacket and tossed it aside, but he grabbed my pants, fell and kept pulling. I heard a seam pop. They were going to rip. One of three pairs I owned. I had to let them go or lose them. He stripped me half-naked, underwear and all. Cock and balls out. Helga and Cecil looked on from the couch, nonplussed. I think Sonny had gone to smoke his joint. Ariadne averted her gaze as she used to at R-rated movies. The other neighbors had said goodnight when Sinatra came on. Let go. You need to let go. He was trying to pull me on the floor. Let go! I lost my sense of humor with my pants. The first punch came down on his head. I started hitting him. I couldn't stop. He wouldn't let go. I was banging his head on the floor. Helga was sitting on the couch. Cecil said he leaned over to her, Is Jimmy Jazz cool with this, or is he mad? He claimed to be listening to Ian Mackay screaming *You'd make a good cop!* Alaska said, though I do sometimes act like a cop, in this case, Cecil had called me to pull Dick off.

I was mad; I was out of control. When I tried to describe how I felt, Alaska said it was shame. I didn't feel ashamed the last time I got in a fight when an opposing soccer dad threatened Ariadne after a game. I didn't feel ashamed when I punched the jock who knocked my video camera over at the Jackie Robinson YMCA while I was taping Black Flag. Is this what it means to be an adult?

I'd somehow got my cock and balls tucked between my legs. Pubic beard like an actor's merkin. Dick was still try-ing to pull me to the floor. Alaska stopped me from really hurting his body. She pried Dick's fingers loose so I could pull my pants up. She'd been in the kitchen washing the dishes. Had cleaned everything while I played songs and continued drinking the last bottle of wine and now Dick was sewing a row of delicate kisses from her wrist to her elbow while she stroked his hair and said, It's alright. It's alright.

I apologized to Helga. I apologized to Ariadne. I may have felt embarrassed being naked in front of my daughter and her boyfriend, but everybody else had seen it before. Cecil had gone to the poetry reading when I stripped nude to shock the host. And Helga had seen me streak out to meet nature head-on inspired by a naked crag of red rock in Utah. Maybe, I wasn't as worried about Ariadne seeing me naked as seeing me at my worst.

Quit navel-gazing.

Dick crawled to the door and Sonny and I helped him down the stairs to the street. He was able to walk with help.

Put your hands on the wall and hold yourself while Helga gets the car, Sonny told him. Sonny used the bouncer voice he'd perfected working the door at Sparky's and Dick complied. Like most ordinary people he'd been beaten into compliance. The clutches and gestures stopped; he'd lost the will to communicate. We put him in the back seat. Buckled him in. Alaska stuffed a plastic bag inside a paper bag in case he had to vomit. She set it on his lap and we closed the door. We should install seatbelts in the couch.

We left you with a dumb, blissful smile on your face, I told him two days later when he brought fresh-cut flowers as a peace offering.

Well, I'm a happy drunk.

Sorry that I'm not.

We drank coffee and ate pumpkin pie.

After I came back from The Crack Den, after Ariadne came back in, in fact about a half-hour after when we were still cleaning up and Armand called from his house to say he was okay, and Helga called to say she was okay and that she'd pulled the car on the lawn and thrown a blanket over Dick in the back seat, we made a decision, a rare family consensus, to visit our parents next Thanksgiving.

# THE GIRL WHO'D NEVER TURNED A CARTWHEEL

Mommy my butt twitches, the girl says. She's about eight, with skinny legs and a big round tummy. Her mother says, Did you wipe? Yes, Mommy, I wiped. Come into the bathroom; let me see. The girl drops her shorts, peels her underpants. Her mother separates the butt cheeks, wads a ball of toilet paper, and mops it. Ow. It still twitches. As mom begins to toss the brown-streaked toilet paper into the toilet, she notices something moving. My god. You have worms. Strangely, it's the mother who feels dirty, like she failed, somehow, which doesn't keep her from telling this story, from spreading the news which passed like a secret from parent to parent around the neighborhood.

## LUXURY HIGH-PERFORMANCE SEDAN

Around midnight we leave Canter's since Barry isn't getting laid even though we'd seen Rodney Bingenheimer and things are looking up. Hustwit says, Mr. Jazz, you're in charge as he hands me the keys to The Luxury High-Performance Sedan, a ridiculous car, by the way, to shuttle a pair of underground beat writers from LA to San Francisco to do a reading from their books. It takes less than an hour to put LA behind us, as we stare into 300 miles of unforgiving highway. Man, it's dark out here, I say stating the obvious. I'm cool to drive for a couple of hours. My camerados have nestled into the soft leather interior and seem to be stretching out into the ample legroom. A feeling of calm cascades over me. The radio is off. The engine makes no sound my blown out ears can hear, the suspension makes me feel like we are floating over the road. It doesn't feel like moving even though the cruise control is set on eighty-five. After about an hour, I dream a parallel road.

Anybody gotta pee?

Two sleepy voices mumble Yes, so I pull to the shoulder. It's cold enough we can see the steam rise from our piss at the side of the highway. Barry says he'll drive, which is fine since it was his idea to leave in the middle of the night. It doesn't take long for him to get the LHS to 110, testing what it can do. I look over and he's squinting through the steering wheel. There are no lights out here, no other cars on the road. I try to ignore it, to sleep, but he keeps tapping the brakes, which causes the vehicle to jerk at a regular rhythm.

Can you slow down? my friend Bill Auto asks from the back seat.

Fuck you, ya wee cunt.

Slow down dude. I was in an accident about a year ago where the car flipped over.

I know how ta drive.

Yeah, he's had a license for a whole year, I say.

Okay ya pussies, Barry says slowing to ninety. He digs around in his duffle bag and produces a pair of dark glasses. The new moon was up there, offering nothing, above the tule fog, which was closing in on the road like the zipper to a body bag.

What are you doing man? You look like Ray Charles.

I forgot my regular speckies, he says. So it's these.

Fuck you, Mr. Magoo, Seymour says from the back.

Even if he could see, the fog has limited visibility to the headlamps. I can't make out more than one white line on the asphalt before it vanishes and another appears. We are hurtling through a tunnel-dark abyss into the unknown. Whenever I'm driving at night and there aren't other cars around, I feel like we got killed in a crash and the afterlife is a road that goes on forever.

I'm serious dude, slow down. If a cow wanders into the road we're dead, Bill says.

What's that eh? Barry stomps the brake pedal, thinking he saw one of Bill's cows in the road, and the purple LHS spins west to the ocean, south to LA, east to desolation screeching to a cold stop. We exhale.

Hey pull over to the shoulder, I gotta piss, ese. When Barry gets out to stretch, I skip the piss and slip into the driver's seat. Fuck you, man. Living is better than sleeping. A light rain starts to fall. We arrive at six am, realizing our friends in the city don't get out of bed before noon. There is very little to do in San Francisco at this hour we discover, but settle in for green tea and toast with marmalade at a café in Chinatown.

## LESS THAN PURPLE

A 767 slams into the World Trade Center like a cock into a vagina. My senses have been arrested like swarthy males at airports. A 767 slams the Pentagon like a cock into an asshole.

On the morning after, the whole country is stunned. It's like a hangover that gets worse when you see who you're in bed with. You remember entering the yuppie piano bar, crocked beyond cognition. First you realize you're not in your own bed, next that you are not in a bed. A small crowd claps, some guys shake their heads and laugh with their bellies. Dat was some fucked up shit homie. I decide not to let the terrorists alter my routine. I turn on my computer [click humm zz-zz-zz] wait for it to boot. The screen blooms from a spore of light. The modem connects to the internet, I wait. [beep beep beep boop -kkkkkkkk] Another three seconds pass while my internet browser launches. Finally I key the phrase http://www.tit4tit.com. Enter. At the top of the screen there's a single square inch pic of what appears to be a sphincter, animated, yawning, pulsing like a beating heart. I scroll past three banner ads extolling pornographic commerce. Mature fatties and grannies. Grow your cock three inches in three days. The money launderers laugh their cynical laughs.

M-Theory

Teen

Pregnant

Asian

Blonde

Puffy

Retro

Petite

Teen

Group

Upskirt

Latina

Gay

Amateur

Ebony

I run the mouse over the categories looking for the funniest site name: big_floppy_titties dot com, boninindamoanin dot com. The site names change daily, but the pictures stay the same. All porn is the same. My coffee smells good, I take a sip. It's hot. I like it black, but I don't like the ebony sites, which seem to be designed by and for rednecks. They show the girls taking two, three, four dicks at once. Jism running out of mouths. I have but one dick. Sites like drunkslut and japbitch don't turn me on.

I click on the bookmark for nytimes dot com. There's a picture of a jet hitting the Trade Center. If I turn on the TV, I can watch it blow up again and again. They say kids think we're being attacked again and again, but I've never met a kid that dumb. Right away people are saying Usama bin Laden. Notice how the first three letters spell USA. Usama. He's our mother, his grandfather invented the zero. Dr. Evil. Changeling, doppelgänger with a knife in every shadow. The base of all problems. I go to MSNBC's website and read an article about how Osama, spelled with an O over here, was set up in the terror business by the CIA. I move from site to site reading about black boxes, cell phone calls from the plane over Pittsburgh and about the heroes trapped under the rubble. Bush II says, It's a crusade to find those folks dead or alive. He thinks he's a cowboy. The Kennebunkport cowboy.

The radio says the number one search string on internet has gone from "sex" to "flag." I clicked on a site once where a girl inserted the eagle that topped a toy flag inside herself. She was a real patriot. Emma Goldman warned in 1908 that patriotism lead to the "bloody specter, militarism." American flags materialize on one of ten cars and in my neighbors' windows. Congress says display the flag to show solidarity. Kim's had her bedroom curtain cracked open enough for the past two months to see pieces of her: a naked hip bone, a bush shaved into a racing stripe. I saw a cock once, accidentally. She must have been having a one-night stand. Now she's hung a red, white, and blue construction paper flag over the opening.

I'm not horny at all. The TV keeps showing people leaping out of 100th floor office windows. Someone said a hot chick got naked before she jumped, but I haven't seen it. The censorship has begun. It won't be long until someone figures how to capitalize on the tragedy. A guy on the radio explains why he needs a million dollars to invent and produce the Skyscraper Office Parachute. If everyone had an SOP in their desk drawers, those people would be alive right now.

About one o'clock, I click on one of those Korean sites where you can watch women eat in front of their webcams. We have lunch together.

After lunch, I can't decide whether I should check the news or look at porn. I still don't feel like looking at porn, but it's been my habit for so long my fingers key in the url for the porn site, like a horse running to the stable. A horse with a three-foot cock. I don't look at bestiality sites; I feel bad for the animals. Masturbating is like falling off a bicycle, once you do it, you never forget. Same banner ads, only now there's an animated gif of an American flag at the top of the page. Jesus fucking christ, even the porn site is waving the flag.

I go to the Times, but they aren't telling me anything. When I was watching the Fox network this conservative dude said there are liberal professors out there who are traitors and should be locked up before they can bad-mouth the USA. I don't understand that. I mean, if the government or the CIA does something bad, what should you do? Keep quiet? Buy something? He also said we need a missile defense system and tax cuts for the wealthy to stimulate the economy. I wondered if he was generalizing or had a specific professor in mind. I realized he was talking about Chomsky. How could I forget? Chomsky is as hard to come by as good free porn. Finding a statement by Noam about The War Against Terror would be like clicking onto a blowjob site to see a girl with a pretty face sucking a dick that looked like mine, same curvature, skin tone, signifying freckle, thickness. The girls on those sites have greasy faces and stringy hair. Never look at a porn site called gravy girls dot com. Chomsky will tell me something. Before I find Chomsky I find Michael Moore. He made that movie Roger & Me and says airport security is a joke. He says the terrorists should have bombed Irvine. Was that a joke? I've been to Irvine and there's not much to bomb. I find Chomsky on counterpunch dot com. Usually this time of the afternoon I look at pictures of lissome teenage girls and play with myself. I've got to get that rotten seed out. But now I'm reading a political tract from an MIT professor. About half way through the article I notice my zipper is down and I'm turning my dickhead over between my left thumb and forefinger while my right hand works the mouse. Chomsky says this is a case of the chickens coming home to roost. Who put the X in Malcolm. Booyah! That's what I was thinking. We treat the world so bad, it's bound to come back at us. I notice that blood is rushing into my cock, it's still less than purple, a mingled damask. I keep reading as my dick gets harder. I'm glad there aren't pictures of Chomsky, since I'm a visual learner, creaming on the images—naked shaved pussies, flexed pink anuses, pierced nipples, ginger minge… nothing. On the TV, they show firefighters and construction guys digging through the rubble. One found a naked shaved pussy, one found a pierced navel.

I went to the computer planning to try the porn site, but somebody emailed a picture of the burning WTC with a devil's visage photoshopped into the smoke. This I find perverse. There's also an email saying to check out an article by Ayn Colter, a buxom blonde, like the ones on tubby cheerleaders dot com. I can't tell whether her tits are firmer than those sagging sacks on Dr. Laura. She says we should invade Afghanistan and convert them to Christianity. She's a little fatter than I go for (give me a break, I've been operantly conditioned by teen sites where girls weigh ninety-five pounds). I can't discern if she has implants through the dowdy blouse her stylist gave her to wear. I think implants are boring. There's something stuck to the head of my dick, which I pick off with my fingernail. If she was here, I would wipe whatever it was on her face and tell her to shut up with the racist crap. She says her best friend was killed on one of the planes. That sucks. Colter goes on and on about what a good woman and wife the dead lady was. Her husband is the lawyer who helped steal the election in that fraud at the Supreme Court. I bet Ayn Colter goes to console him and he gets caught with his dick in her mouth. It says in the bible a woman should swallow every drop of semen. I bet he licks her anus while she imagines swarthy males invading Connecticut to rape her.

My dick is out, hard. I've got the skin gripped and am jerking it up and down as I read. This conservative porn isn't doing it, even though it comes with pictures. I click the mouse and the Counterpunch page starts to load. White background. Black text. Word after word. My left hand forgets about my cock, which hangs out of the slit in my filthy boxer shorts. I should get to the Laundromat. I'm conscious of the sweat underneath my balls as I read. I'm learning a lot already about the Mujahideen, the CIA sponsored terror against the Soviets, tit for tit Israeli and Palestinian violence. The IRA and the UDA are still at it too, but no one's shooting Cruise missiles at Belfast. Before I realize it my cock is stiff and I can feel the load of cum like rainwater behind a dam. My sperm are anxious as thoroughbreds in the gate. All it would take is a few strokes. I let my finger turn circles in the tears. But do I want to train myself to have orgasms by reading left-wing political treatises?

I wonder if my apprehension is a crisis of faith. At least I'm paying attention. At least I'm conducting business as usual. But the president said go buy stuff. Maybe I should apply for salon dot com premium content. It's thirty dollars a year to access the news and politics sections. I've never paid for internet porn. Uhh huh huh.

Jimmy Carter and Zbigniew Brzezinski funded the Mujahideeee! Oh, oh uhhh! Ahhhh. Some of the spunk hit the monitor. That's never happened. Intense. I'm shaking. At the same time, I feel a spiritual calm I haven't known since before 911. Most of the semen is dripping on my hand. It smells clean. I should get into a chat room and tell someone.

The next morning I go to Counterpunch. They have a link to Mother Jones, The Nation, Cursor, and a dozen other free political speech sites. Maybe I'll become an anarchist, it says here anarchists don't have to buy anything. If the economy collapses my life won't change much. Chomsky has posted a new interview. I feel the blood rush to my brain.

# GOVERNED BY SUPERSTITION

I shouldn't have known it was midnight, but I woke up. Alaska woke too. Did you hear something? Did you? Yeah. We could argue whether it was a bump or a rustling but there's no doubt it came from the kitchen. It may have been our cat knocking something over; she's known to tip forgotten cups. A sound perceived on either side of consciousness. We listen with intent though neither wants to get out of bed. My eyes adjust to the plastic gray city night dark; the glowing red letters of the digital clock read 12:00. The alarm will jolt us awake five hours hence. They say people who get eight hours of sleep are healthier, as Alaska likes to remind. And she's already gone back, each breath growing heavier. I lie awake, drifting in a drunken boat... RREEE-OWW! This noise, for sure, is my cat. I leap out of bed. Hissssss! Jesus fucking Christ. I throw the light on, squint, see Alaska erect, pale as an unearthed Greek statue, with the down comforter pulled across her bare chest. Our cat, Fobos, stands with claws flexed at the edge of the bed puffed three times her size, her vicious hiss shifting octaves into a low rumbling growl rrrrrr pointed under the bed. My imagination runs. Homunculus? Rat? Roach? Crow ....Mouse? We had a mouse once but Fobos, heedless, watched it carry a crumb from the refrigerator to the stove. I flip the blanket and see an ugly too beat calico, scabby-faced, hairless in patches, missing whiskers, a knick outta the ear, scoliotic spine, shivering with a hollow near-imperceptible growl bubbling in her own deep throat. John Ashcroft, Attorney General of the United States, said calico cats were emissaries of the Devil—like the witches lining up to kiss the master's arse calico cats are all female. Ashcroft once lost an election to a dead guy, gotta love cynical American voters. He covered the breasts on the Statue of Justice too. Surprised he didn't bag her haughty head and mug for a photo. How'd this cat get in here? We look around the apartment, all three windows shut against the cold. In the kitchen, I find the broom closet ajar, do a quick review of the facts: unexplained bump, closet open, the upstairs neighbor we never talk to has a cat. Dumbshit dumped the litter box in the recycling bin. We call her Humpy Humpalot because… well… a preponderance of evidence. The cat must have fallen through a hole in the ceiling inside the broom closet. Sounds right, I say. Cats land on their feet. I throw a blanket over the haggard crone and lock her in the bathroom. Before I switch off the light, Alaska uncovers her breasts and welcomes me to bed.

*Photo by Anthony Scoggins*

Jimmy Jazz is a writer from San Diego.

I was born in 1966. I lived with my daughter's mom for 30 years before we got married on our 30th anniversary. I choose day jobs that leave me energy for writing, the best was The Museum of Death. I love books and have a home library with 2,805 volumes. I collect books from small presses like AK, Exact Change, Manic D, Black Sparrow, New Directions, City Lights & Re/Search.

I would say I'm a veteran spoken word artist, fortunate to have shared a stage with many of my favorite writers:

Steve Abee, Linda Albertano, Dave Alvin, Don Bajema, Liz Belile, Iris Berry, Angela Boyce, Derrick Brown, Dennis Cooper, Creedle, Kimberly Dark, Sharon Elise, Maggie Estep, Raymond Federman, Rich Ferguson, Larry Fondation, Weba Garretson, Pleasant Gehman, Gary Glazner, Daphne Gottlieb, Barry Graham, Cecil Hayduke, Stevie Harris, Michael Hemmingson, Stewart Home, Hank Hyena, Tamara Johnson, Shawna Kenney, Michael Klam, The Last Poets, Mary Leary, Beth Lisick, Lob, Jon Longhi, Richard Loranger, Lydia Lunch, Douglas A. Martin, Ellyn Maybe, Larry McCaffery, Jeffrey McDaniel, June Melby, Joe Milosch, minerva, Mindy Nettifee, Matthew Niblock, Alexis O'Hara, Nicole Panter, Peter Plate, Clebo Rainey, El Rivera, La Ruocco, Michelle Serros, Several Girls Galore, Shappy, Bucky Sinister, Hal Sirowitz, The Taco Shop Poets, Jervey Tervalon, Juliette Torrez, Tarin Towers, Quincy Troupe, Chris Vannoy, Lizzie Wann, Pam Ward, Ted Washington, Saul Williams, William Upski Wimsatt & The Watts Prophets. He has performed at The SDSU Avant-garde Festival, The Fringe Fest, SXSW, The National Poetry Slam & Lollapalooza 94.

I have written poetry, short fiction, long fiction & non-fiction. My history of DIY publishing extends to the early 90s, though my novel The Sub was published by Incommunicado Press in 1996. I was chosen by San Diego City College to be the featured writer for their journal City Works in 2002. I spent six years writing The Book of Books which Rich Ferguson called my "magnum opus."